From Around The World

# The Matchless Pearl and other mythical tales

*By*
Swapna Dutta
Ramendra Kumar

*Illustrated by*
Sonal Goyal
Sumit Sakuja



UNICORN BOOKS

**UNICORN BOOKS PVT. LTD.,** New Delhi-110002


***Distributors***
**Pustak Mahal®, Delhi**

J-3/16 , Daryaganj, New Delhi-110002
☎ 23276539, 23272783, 23272784 • *Fax:* 011-23260518
*E-mail:* info@pustakmahal.com • *Website:* www.pustakmahal.com

***Branch Offices***
**Bangalore:** ☎ 22234025
*E-mail*: pmblr@sancharnet.in • pustak@sancharnet.in
**Mumbai:** ☎ 22010941
*E-mail*: rapidex@bom5.vsnl.net.in
**Patna:** ☎ 3094193 • *Telefax:* 0612-2302719
*E-mail*: rapidexptn@rediffmail.com
**Hyderabad:** *Telefax:* 040-24737290
*E-mail*: pustakmahalhyd@yahoo.co.in

ISBN 81-780-6102-3

**Edition : 2006**



printed at United Colours (India)

# Contents

## Swapna Dutta

## Ramendra Kumar

# Betushka's Adventure

(*A story from Czechoslovakia*)

Betushka was a young girl who lived with her mother in a tiny little cottage. They were very poor and just had a few goats. Betushka's father had been a weaver. Now that he was dead, Betushka's mother wove what she could with the thread Betushka spun for her in her little spindle. That is how mother and daughter managed to live.

Although they were very poor yet, Betushka was always happy and cheerful. Every morning she took the goats for grazing to the birch wood nearby. She carried a piece of bread for lunch and her spindle. She spent all day spinning thread from flax as she kept an eye on the goats. She was too poor to buy a distaff on which to wind her flax. So, she wound it around her head when she left for the birch wood every morning.

"See that all this flax is used up and your spindle is full before you return home, Betushka" her mother told her every morning before she set off.

"Yes, mother" Betushka replied cheerfully. She danced behind the goats all the way to the birch wood. Then she sat down under a tree and left the goats to graze. She pulled the fibres from the flax with one hand and twirled her spindle with the other as she sang softly to herself all the time. When it was mid-day and the sun was overhead, Betushka stopped work for a while. She took out her piece of bread and had her lunch, always giving a share to the

goats. After that, since she was still hungry, she picked up wild strawberries from the wood and ate them. Then she got up and danced round the tree so that she might not feel sleepy. After this short break she sat down and spun steadily all afternoon. By the time it was time to go home with the goats, her spindle would be full of flaxen thread.

As Betushka sat spinning one spring afternoon a beautiful maiden appeared before her. Her golden hair, bright and fine as silk, reached down to her ankles. She wore a stately white dress made of the finest lace and a crown made of the loveliest flowers. Betushka had never seen such a beautiful girl before and wondered if she was real. Suddenly the girl asked, "Betushka, do you know how to dance?"

"Of course I do" Betushka replied, "I love dancing more than anything else. But how did you know my name?"

"Then come and dance with me" said the girl smiling at Betushka, "It is a spring afternoon, just the right time for dancing."

She took Betushka's hand and the two of them danced together, going round and round the trees. The birds sang sweetly providing the music for their dancing. Betushka's heart filled with a strange joy as she danced and forgot all about her goats and her spinning. They danced together as long as there was light. As soon as the sun set, the beautiful girl vanished as suddenly as she had come. The birds stopped their song at the same time. Betushka suddenly realised that her spindle was only half full of thread because she had spent the whole afternoon dancing. She was very quiet as she walked back home with her goats. She was sorry she had failed her mother and made up her mind to spin double the amount of thread the next day and to make up for her neglect.

Her mother was surprised to find her so quiet.

"Are you ill, Betushka?" she asked anxiously. "No mother, I am sleepy and tired" said Betushka as she turned in for the night very early, determined to work double the next day. Her mother saw the half-filled spindle when Betushka was asleep but said nothing to her then.

Betushka rushed to the birch wood the next morning and started spinning at once. When it was afternoon she ate her piece of bread quickly and went on spinning again.

"I shall NOT dance today" she told her goats.

"Oh yes, you will" said a laughing voice. It was the same beautiful girl. "Betushka, do come and dance with me."

"I am sorry but I can't" said Betushka, "I must finish my spinning before the sun sets."

"I'll help you finish it" said the girl, "now come and dance."

The birds were singing again. Betushka just could not resist it. She took the girl's hand and they danced round and round.

When the sun was about to set, Betushka suddenly remembered about her spinning and looked at her spindle. It lay on the ground, completely empty. Betushka burst into tears.

"Don't cry Betushka" said the girl, "I always keep my promise."

She took the flax out of Betushka's hair and wound it round a birch tree. Then she took up the spindle and started to spin. How fast she could spin! Before the sun set there was no flax left and the spindle was full of thread. "Take it and never grumble" said the girl and vanished like before, "Remember, never grumble".

Betushka was not quite sure what the girl meant but she took the goats home happily singing all the way. But Betushka's mother was not happy to see the full spindle. She had seen the half empty spindle in Betushka's bag last night and knew that she had not spun much thread the previous day.

"Why did you not complete your spinning yesterday?" she asked Betushka as soon as she returned home.

"I was dancing and forgot the time" said Betushka. But she did not tell her mother about the beautiful girl she had met and danced with.

"Mind you, don't ever do such a thing again" she told Betushka.

"No, mother, I shall not" Betushka promised.

But when Betushka went to the birch wood the next day the beautiful girl appeared again. Betushka forgot all about her promise and danced with her all day. When the sun set and Betushka saw her empty spindle, she started crying again.

"Don't cry, Betushka" said the girl and picked up her bag. When she returned it to Betushka it was full of something light. "I have given you something and your mother will not scold you. But you must not open the bag or see what I have given before you reach home." Then she disappeared as usual.

Betushka meant to keep her word. But she felt so curious about what the beautiful girl had given her that she thought she would just take one small peep inside the bag. When she looked she saw that it was stuffed full of dry birch leaves. Betushka was so hurt and disappointed that she threw most of the leaves away. Then she suddenly remembered that they might come handy for lighing a fire and left the few remaining ones inside.

Betushka was really afraid of what her mother would say this time. Her mother was waiting at the gate. "What did you do to your spindle yesterday?" she asked her, "I kept on and on winding the thread but the spindle remained full. The moment I started grumbling and said that some evil spirit must have done something to the spindle, all the thread simply vanished! Tell me what it means, Betushka. You must have met someone in the birch wood."

Betushka told her mother about the beautiful girl and their dancing.

"That must have been a wood fairy" cried her mother, "they always dance at mid-day. And they give lovely presents to the girls they dance with. Why didn't you tell me about her before? Didn't she give you anything, Betushka?"

"Well, yes, she spun that thread for me yesterday and today she gave me some dry leaves" said Betushka.

"Show them to me" said her mother.

"They were only dry leaves, mother" said Betushka, "I threw away most of them. But there are a few in my bag."

When Betushka opened her bag she found that the dry leaves had turned to gold!

"Silly girl, how could you throw away the rest of the leaves?" cried her mother, "We would have had a bag full of gold!"

"Let us go and find them" said Betushka, "I remember where I threw them."

But when they went back to the wood the next morning, there were only fresh birch leaves in the wood. There were no gold leaves at all, not a single one.

"Never mind, we still have a few gold leaves" said Betushka, "They will buy a lot of things."

"Yes, we must not grumble. No wood fairy will tolerate grumbling" said Betushka's mother, "If only I had not grumbled yesterday I would have had a room full of thread from that spindle."

So Betushka and her mother bought a farm and cattle and a nice cottage with the gold leaves and lived comfortably for the rest of their lives. But Betushka never saw the wood fairy again.

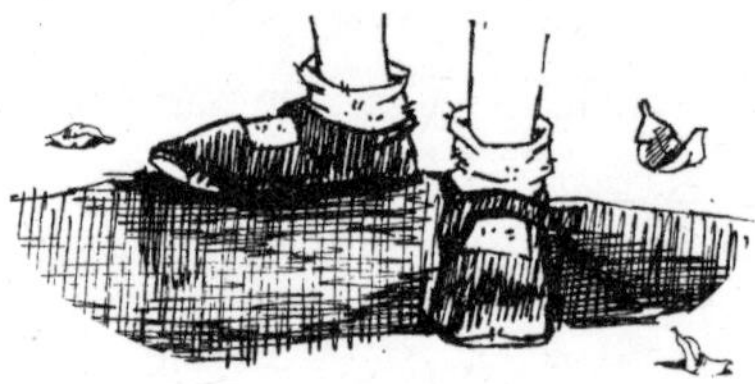

# The Matchless Pearl

*(A story from China)*

Once upon a time there lived a Jade Dragon on the eastern bank of the Celestial River. In the deep, dark forest on the other side of the river lived the Golden Phoenix. The dragon spent most of its time swimming in the river while the phoenix flew about in the sky. But the two were great friends and met each other every day.

One day the Jade Dragon and the Golden Phoenix decided to visit the fairy island together. As they went exploring they found a pretty little pebble that shone brightly in the sunlight.

"Look how pretty the pebble is!". cried the phoenix.

"Let us polish it and turn it into a pearl" said the dragon. They picked it up and took it away with them. The dragon polished it with his claws while the phoenix polished it with her beak. They were at it day after day. The phoenix scooped up dew drops in her beak to clean the pebble. The dragon fetched water from the Celestial River. They washed and polished the pebble with dew and water until it turned into a beautiful, matchless pearl.

The dragon and the phoenix loved the pearl that they had created. And they also loved each other. So, they decided to settle down in the fairy island and guard the pearl. They did not realise that it was a magic pearl. Things bloomed and blossomed wherever it shone. The grass grew greener, the flowers more colourful and fragrant, and the crops bright and golden.

One morning as the queen of heaven passed by she saw the pearl sparkling in the fairy island. She had never seen anything so wonderful before. She decided to take it away and sent one of her guards to steal it in the dead of night when the dragon and the phoenix were asleep. She was delighted when the guard returned with it and locked it up in her innermost chamber. One had to pass nine doors to reach it. The queen put big locks on all the nine doors and kept the keys carefully.

When the dragon and the phoenix woke up the next morning, they were heartbroken to find that their precious pearl had been stolen. The dragon searched all along the Celestial River, looking into every nook and cranny of the river bed while the phoenix combed every inch of the Sacred Mountain. But their pearl was nowhere to be found.

After some months, it was the birthday of the queen of heaven. All the Gods and Goddesses arrived at her palace to wish her. She had prepared a grand feast and entertained them lavishly. Then one of the guests said, "Oh queen, I wish I could get you a precious gift that can neither be found in heaven or on earth."

The queen laughed at the words and said, "I do have such an object and it is more precious than any of my jewels."

"Can we see it please?" the guests asked eagerly.

The queen then opened the nine doors and fetched the pearl from the innermost chamber.

"Here it is. Isn't it beautiful?" The entire hall lit up with the light from the pearl. The guests stared at it fascinated.

The dragon and the phoenix were still searching for their treasure when the phoenix suddenly saw the bright glow of their pearl lighting up the enormous hall of heaven.

"Look, look, isn't that the light of our own pearl?" Phoenix asked excitedly.

"Indeed it is" said the dragon, "Let us go there and get it back."

They flew towards the light – the phoenix carrying the dragon and found themselves in the banquet hall of the queen. Their pearl lay on the table, while all the guests were gazing at its brilliance.

“This is our pearl” cried the Jade Dragon.

“This is our pearl” cried the Golden Phoenix.

“Nonsense” snapped the queen of heaven, “Everything on earth and heaven belongs to me, including this pearl.”

“But this pearl does not belong to either earth or heaven. It did not grow there. We created it from a mere pebble after years of hard work” said the dragon and the phoenix together.

The queen ordered her guards to throw out the dragon and the phoenix. But they fought hard and dashed back to take away the pearl. While they were fighting, the pearl slipped from the table, rolled down the stairs and fell into space. Everyone knew that it would soon crash down on the earth and break into pieces. The dragon and the phoenix rushed out and flew towards the falling pearl, trying to catch it before it fell down. But they did not succeed. The pearl fell on earth and immediately turned into a clear, green lake. The Jade Dragon and the Golden Phoenix could not bear to leave it. So both of them turned into two big mountains and remained forever by the lake which was named “West Lake” by the people. The dragon and the phoenix came to be known as the Jade Dragon Mountain and the Golden Phoenix Mountain, which stand by the West Lake in China to this day.

# The Lake that Found a New Home

*(A story from Estonia)*

Do you know where Estonia is? It is a country in northeastern Europe which is made up of a mainland and more than 1,500 islands in the Baltic Sea. These islands are full of lakes, some small and some big. This story is about a big lake called the Eim.

Eim was a big and beautiful lake with clear, blue water. It had tall trees growing all round. By and by more and more trees grew there making a deep and dense forest. Gradually the forest became the home of many kinds of birds and animals. No, there were no tigers and lions or wild elephants as we have in our forests here. But there were other animals – elk and roe, deer and red deer, wild boars and bears, lynx and many others which love to live near the sea. And along with all these animals the forest also became the den of wicked robbers. They came here because it was an excellent place to hide and also hide all their loot.

The people of the land knew that the robbers lived here and did not come anywhere near the forest if they could help it! Of course they missed the beautiful Eim Lake where they used to boat and swim and fish before the forest grew so dark and thick. But, they did not come near it now because they were afraid of the robbers. The robbers were known to be dangerous killers as well.

As a matter of fact, they thought nothing of killing! They shot down birds and animals whenever they wanted meat. They went fishing in the lake when they felt like eating fish. But there was

another reason as well or they might never have bothered to fish. People of Estonia believed that the bed of the Lake Eim was full of gold belonging to an earlier civilization. *(That land of plenty was drowned when Lake Eim was created.)* The people died, their palaces were immersed in the lake water and their treasures lay scattered on the bed of the lake. But the lake was so deep that no one dared to dive down and get them. Not even these robbers, though some of them were good swimmers. So they merely kept fishing and angling in the lake hoping that they might be able to pick up something precious.

Lake Eim was not at all happy about having the robbers living so near it. The lake did not mind their fishing or boating. But it felt really annoyed because they made the water so dirty. They never dredged the shallow parts of the lake like other people did. Or bothered to clear the weeds that were beginning to grow all around the lake. They never even bothered to cut the nettles that sprang up wild and unchecked. The robbers were terribly lazy and hated the thought of doing any kind of hard work. And needless to say, they didn't mind living amidst dirt.

Although the robbers grew lazier by the day, their craving for money did not grow any less. At first they merely used to rob the passers-by and gave them a few knocks. But as they grew more and more wicked and more desperate for money, they started killing the passers-by after looting them. Then they would simply throw their bodies into the lake. Their blood stained the water and the lake simply hated it. Before long, the water grew dirty and started smelling of blood! Even the flowers that grew by the lakeside got blood stains on them. The weeds and grass rotted and the mud along the lakeside got frothy. But the wicked robbers did not care! They did not even notice how the beautiful lake was gradually changing into something repulsive and ugly. At last Lake Eim could bear it no more and decided to fly away to another country.

That night, a strange noise woke up the leader of the robbers. He sat up and rubbed his eyes. The forest was usually so silent at night. What on earth was happening? What was the strange and loud scraping sound? It sounded as if someone was trying to scraping off something from the ground. Then he suddenly felt splashes of water falling on him. Could it be raining? But the sky was full of stars and he could see a pale, round moon on the horizon. By then the entire group of robbers was up.

'What's the matter, boss?' they asked, 'What's that strange noise?'

'And where's the water coming from? It isn't raining. There's the moon!'

'What's happening to the lake?' cried another, 'Just turn round and see!'

Every eye was on the lake. But good gracious, where was the lake? They saw something that made their hair stand on end! The lake was rolling itself up like a huge carpet, shaking off the mud that clung to the bottom with a loud scraping noise. Then it rose straight up like a huge glittering tent. They could see an enormous sheet of water spread across the sky holding millions and millions of gallons of water. Would it break on top of them and drown them all? The robbers clutched one another and shook in fear. They did not know that the lake was disgusted with the place and was flying away to a different land. It swirled across the sky and was soon out of sight.

None of the robbers could sleep that night. They simply clutched one another in fear and stood staring at the sky. Was it a bad dream? Would everything be as before once it was light? But when the sun rose the next morning, there was no lake Eim. Instead, the robbers saw a huge hole full of slush where the lake had been.

'Come along, boys!' cried the leader of the robbers excitedly, 'The place must be teeming with all the treasure we have been looking for all these months. How wonderful that there is no water and we can get it all.'

'But our boats are all gone' said one of the robbers, looking at the river bed.

'Who wants boats?' said the leader, 'there's no lake now and no water. We can just walk in and pick up the treasure.'

'I can see the treasure chests gleaming in the sun – many, many of them' cried another robber excitedly.

"Remember to take a net and grab all the fish' said the leader, 'they must be there in the mud and will provide us wonderful meals.'

The robbers jumped in and were soon up to their waists in mud. But there were no fish to be seen!

'The lake must have taken them when it flew away' said the leader. 'Never mind, we can take all the treasure.'

'Luckily the chests are all open,' said one of the robbers putting his hands in. He was expecting to pick up a handful of gold coins or some wonderful jewellery. But, something stung him and he screamed and pulled his hands out. The chest was full of snakes! The other chests were full of frogs and lizards, newt, salamander, slugs and other slimy creatures that wrapped themselves around the robbers and bit them hard. The robbers screamed and ran for the shore. But, the snakes and lizards, slugs and frogs followed them to the shore and got into their huts, their clothes, their beds and all their things. It was like a nightmare! They ran all over the place but could not escape the vicious creatures.

'The only thing we can do now is to set fire to our huts or these creatures will kill us' said the leader.

'What about all our stolen goods and money?' cried the others, 'if we set fire to our huts all that we have collected in all these months will be burnt to ashes.'

'Staying alive is more important than anything else. What use will all our stolen wealth be if the creatures kill us first?' said the leader.

The entire forest was soon reduced to a mass of flames. The burnt trees made a charred ring around the empty crater. The robbers trudged away empty-handed, badly bitten and burnt. They could save nothing of their ill-gotten goods.

By this time the Lake Eim had flown a long way across the sky and was just wondering what to do when it saw a stretch of dry, parched land. The mud was brown and cracked. There was hardly any vegetation and no water in the dry river beds and empty ponds. The villagers saw the lake in the sky and thought it was a strange and special cloud.

'Oh please give us a few drops of water' they begged, 'we are dying for want of water and our crops have perished too.'

'Why is there no water here?" asked Lake Eim curiously.

'Because we have had a severe drought, the like of which we have never known before' replied the people. 'We are dying of thirst and our fields have all dried up.'

Lake Eim felt sorry for them.

'I shall come down and stay with you if you can make a bed for me to lie on' it told them in a thundering voice.

'Oh we will, we will!' they cried in a chorus, 'please, please stay with us.'

After that the entire village started working. How they worked! The men dug the empty soil with their spades and trowels. The children dug with their bare hands. The women wheeled away the earth in barrows. Others carried them away in pans and basins. Before the week was out, they had dug a huge bed for the lake to lie in. Lake Eim crept down from the sky and lay down happily. Its water had turned crystal clear once again. And the lake had carried all the fish, boats and all the treasure with it. As the waves gently lapped the shores, Eim threw bits of gold and silver on the sands. The villagers cheered as they picked them up and caught the boats that had once belonged to the wicked robbers.

All the people of this land – men, women and children - knelt down along the shore and thanked the lake for choosing to stay with them and for giving them so much. They planted trees all around the lake and cleaned up the entire shore. They built jetties for their boats and dug troughs for their cattle. They dug channels to carry water to their fields. They made a shallow pool beside the lake where children could play and swim and built seats near the water where old people could sit and rest. They went fishing and picked up both fish and bits of silver and gold. The water from the lake helped them grow their crops and the place was soon green with new trees. Flowers bloomed and birds sang and everyone was happy. Lake Eim looked at its new home and sighed with contentment.

# How the Sea was Created

*(A story from Melanesia)*

There are many legends about how the sea was created. One of them is from Melanesia.

Melanesia is one of the three large groups of islands in the Pacific Ocean that are collectively known as "Oceania". The islands lie northeast of Australia. Melanesia is made up of the islands of Fiji, New Caledonia, New Guinea, Solomon Islands and Vanuatu.

The story goes that long , long ago there were no oceans. There were deserts and vast open spaces, green fields, rocky patches and mountains. And there were rivers and lakes. If people wanted to go fishing, swimming or boating, that is where they went.

Somewhere near the bottom of a steep hill in Melanesia was a tiny little pool, well hidden among the bushes that grew there. It was so small that you could easily jump across it. The water of the pool was a clear blue. A woman who lived nearby discovered the pool accidentally one day when she came near the hill to collect firewood. As she looked at the pool in surprise and saw the clear blue water, she remembered that she was thirsty. She tried to drink the water but found it salty. But although she did not feel like drinking the water, she rather liked the taste of salt and guessed it would make her cooking tastier. She had nothing to carry the water in just then. So she went back home. But she returned the next day with a bucket and carried the salty water home. She cooked a stew with the same water and waited to see what her family would say.

"What wonderful stew!" said her husband. "How come it tastes so different this evening? What did you put into it?"

"Mama, the stew tastes lovely" added her first son. "It's very different from your usual cooking. I wonder why."

"I can *see* nothing different" said her second son, "it has the same carrots, turnips, potatoes, beans and pieces of meat. Why does it taste so different?"

"I really can't say. It tastes the usual to me" said the woman.

She had already made up her mind to keep the pool a secret. She didn't want other prying eyes discovering it and taking the special water away. She was afraid that her naughty sons would mess about in the pool and make the water dirty and tell the entire village about it. So she told them nothing. But she continued to go to the pool every day and fetch a bucket of water for her cooking. She took care to go there at a time when no one was around. She took a piece of cloth with her the next time and covered up the pool completely. She also put stones on the edges so that the cloth might not blow away with the wind.

Her two sons were very curious. They soon guessed that their mother had a secret. They also guessed that it had something to do with her cooking and the water she cooked with. The water looked very ordinary and so did the bucket. Since they did not taste it, they did not know it was salty. But when the pan was dry they noticed a fine white powder at the bottom.

"Where do you get your water from, mama?" asked the elder son.

"From where I got it all these years" she replied, "why do you ask?"

"May we go with you the next time you go to fetch it?" asked the second son.

"No" she said at once.

"Why not? I shall carry the bucket for you" said the first son. "You can take along a bigger bucket if you like."

"There is no need" said the woman. "Go and help your father in the field instead. Don't bother me."

The boys left her alone. But they were now convinced that their mother was keeping something from them. They decided to follow her secretly the next time and find out what it was. When she went out to fetch water from the pool the next day, they followed her at a distance. When they came close to the hill they climbed up a tree to see what she was doing. But the trees grew close together and they could see nothing. After some time they saw their mother coming out of the woods with the bucket of water.

"Strange!" said the first brother. "There's no river or pond in there. Where did mama get the water from?"

"Let's go and explore after she has gone home" said the second brother.

They climbed down from the tree and went inside the wood at the foot of the hill. They could see nothing at first. No river, no lake, no pond or even a well. Where did their mother take the water from? Was there a hidden spring or pool in the forest? They started searching for one, going over the entire place very carefully. Finally they came to the little pool.

"Here is a sheet covering the grass" said the first brother. "How funny! Who did it and why?"

"Pick it up and see. Perhaps there is something hidden underneath" said the second brother. They pulled off the sheet and found the little pool below.

"Pooh! Just a tiny puddle!" said the first brother, "Must have been made by the rain". "Taste the water and see. It looks very blue. I wonder why. Puddles usually have muddy water in them" said the second brother.

The first brother scooped up a palmful of water and tasted it. He made a face and spat it out. "It tastes awful!" he said, "horrid little puddle!"

As soon as he spoke these words and spat out the water, there came a strange hissing sound from the pool. The water gushed up like a fountain and drenched the two brothers.

"Look what you have done!" cried the second brother. "You shouldn't have called the pool names!"

"You made me taste it" said the first brother.

In the mean time, the water from the pool started rising higher and higher and spreading all over the place. The brothers soon found themselves in a vast lake of water with the water steadily rising above their ankles, to their waist, to their neck and higher. Both brothers ran in two different directions in panic but the water followed them. The deep blue salty water swished and gurgled and turned into rolling breakers, breaking on every side, sweeping away cows and goats, houses and trees and everything that came in the way. There were vast sheets of water all around and huge big waves everywhere.

Finally, the water reached the village where the mother of the boys stood shivering looking at the gushing water. She saw it rushing towards her like a huge big wall. She ran out into the garden and broke some twigs from a tree and planted them in a straight line whispering some magic chants. The water broke all over her and for a while she was under it, struggling to stand up. But when the water touched the line of twigs she had planted, it started receding gradually. It did not go beyond the twigs so there was some land left beyond. But the water rushed all around it. Before long there was only a small island left with a vast sea surrounding it and other small islands that raised their heads above the water here and there. These were the different islands of Melanesia. And the ocean has covered a large part of the world ever since.

# The Devil's Gift

*(A story from Norway)*

Long, long ago there lived two brothers. The elder one was rich and had everything that money could buy. He had a huge house full of servants, a garden full of flowers, fruits and vegetables, grand clothes, horses and carriages and enough money to do whatever he wanted. The younger brother was very poor. He lived in a tumbledown cottage that was icy cold in winter and hot and stuffy in summer. All he had was a rugged little field that yielded very little crop so he could barely manage to have two square meals a day.

The elder brother, despite having so much, was mean and selfish and hated to share his wealth with anyone else. He took no notice of his brother who led such a miserable life next door.

It was the time of Easter and everyone in the country was merry making. The elder brother was having a big party in his house where he had called everyone except his brother and his family. The younger brother who had eaten nothing for the last few days decided to go and beg for some leftovers from his elder brother. He knew that he would not be welcome at his house but at least he could bring something to feed his family.

"Please give me something to eat" he pleaded, "My wife and children are hungry. In return I promise to do whatever you ask me."

The elder brother was very annoyed to see him. But when the younger brother kept on pleading he picked up a piece of bread from the table, buttered it and threw it to him. "There!" he said, "Take that and go to the devil! And don't ever dare to come back here."

The younger brother picked up the piece of bread. He was about to rush back home when he remembered that he had promised to do whatever his brother asked him. He did not know where the devil lived but he had to find it somehow before he took the piece of bread home. He walked on and on, asking people the way as he went, and finally reached the devil's door. The devil was just taking his after-dinner walk by the gate. He was surprised to see a stranger outside.

"Who are you? And what's that you are holding?" he asked curiously.

"It's a buttered piece of bread" said the younger brother.

"It looks delicious. Why don't you give it to me? I'd like to taste it" said the devil.

"It's all I have and I must share it with my family for dinner" said the younger brother.

"Never mind that" said the devil smacking his lips, "You give me the bread and I shall give you a magic wheel. The wheel will give you whatever you ask for. So you will not remain poor any longer."

The younger brother gave him the bread and thanked him for the magic wheel. "But you must also teach me how to make it stop. I wouldn't want the wheel to go on and on!" The devil laughed. "You are a clever fellow. Most people would not remember to ask me that." He taught the magic chant which would make the wheel work and the chant that would make it stop as he handed him the wheel. He thanked the devil once again for his kindness and started for home.

His wife was very worried and was wondering what could have happened, when the younger brother walked in with the magic wheel. "Where have you been?" she cried, "And you have brought us no food. Are we to go to the bed hungry even on Easter night?"

"Don't worry, you will soon have all the goodies you want to have and more" said the younger brother as he set the wheel on the table. "Wheel, give us a wonderful dinner" he said, repeating the magic chant. In a moment the table was full of the most delicious dishes – soup, meat, poultry, eggs, fish, bread and buns galore, puddings and pies. And of course there was the special delicacy of Norway – soup and herrings. Everyone stuffed themselves until they could eat no more. Then the wheel provided them with new clothes and soft, warm beds with cosy blankets. They went to sleep wondering if all this was a dream and if they would find themselves in their cold and dreary room when it was morning. But nothing changed. Soon the younger brother was as rich and prosperous as his elder brother and had everything that he wanted.

The news that the younger brother now had a grand place of his own soon reached the elder brother. He did not believe it at first. But, when he went to check it out for himself he was amazed to see the change in his brother's condition.

"Who gave you all this money?" he asked his brother.

"The wheel" said the younger brother pointing to the wheel on the shelf.

"Rubbish! I don't believe you!" said the elder brother. "You'd better tell me where you got your wealth from or I'll make you sorry."

"I'm telling you, it's all because of the wheel" said the younger brother. "Wait, I'll show you how it works." He fetched the wheel and placed it on the table. "Wheel, let me have some wonderful fruits" he ordered. In a moment the table was full of luscious fruits.

The elder brother simply snatched the wheel from the younger brother and walked away. "I am the elder. The wheel should rightfully belong to me" he said. The younger brother shrugged and smiled.

"I shall soon surprise everyone" said the elder brother to himself. After reaching home, he asked his wife to go and supervise the workers in the fields. He then placed the wheel on his table and said, "Wheel, let me have soup and herrings. Plenty of it." The wheel obediently started pouring soup and herrings in the big soup tureen. Once the tureen was full, it went on pouring soup in all the other containers including tubs and buckets. "Stop, stop. I don't want any more" said the elder brother, "You have given us enough to feed an army!" But the wheel did not stop! One needed to say a special magic chant to make it stop and the elder brother did not know it. The wheel continued to pour more and more soup until the entire house was full of it. Very soon the soup rose to the level of the windows and started flowing out. Before long there was a river of soup with big waves where the herrings floated and everything in the house flew out with it. "Stop, stop!" cried the elder brother again and again. "I shall soon lose everything and my house will be ruined." But the magic wheel did not stop and turned the place into a lake of soup where the elder brother's house, gardens, orchards and stables were all drowned.

The elder brother swam along the river of soup and reached his younger brother's house.

"Please save me from the wheel and make it stop" he pleaded. The wheel had also come floating behind him. The younger brother picked it up and whispered the magic chant. Instantly it stopped pouring out soup. But the lake and river of soup remained, though it soon grew lighter and turned to water.

"You should not have snatched the wheel from me" said the younger brother. "I would have willingly given it to you if only you had asked for it."

"I don't want your wheel" said the elder brother with a shudder. "But my house and everything is ruined. What shall I do now?"

"I shall give you a new house and enough money to rebuild a new life. But please try to be a little less selfish in future and try to share things with others" said the younger brother. "And now that we both have enough, I think I shall return the devil's gift" he said to himself, "I don't want to be too greedy and ruin my life!"

The elder brother left with the money and built a house far away from the younger brother. He wasn't going anywhere near the terrible wheel and risk his life again!

# Saint George and the Dragon

*(A story from Libya)*

Some of you may know that Saint George is considered the patron saint of England. There are many stories about him. The best known among them is the story of how he killed a dangerous dragon. This story, translated into English in the 12$^{th}$ century, is known as one of the "Golden Legends".

Long, long ago at the town of Silene in Libya, there ruled a king who had a beautiful daughter named Sabra. He had a prosperous kingdom by a lake, devoted and loyal subjects, and everything that a king could wish for. But one day, something dreadful happened that ruined it all and drowned the entire kingdom in terror. A terrible dragon entered the kingdom and made its home in the lake. It was the most dreadful monster you can imagine and was as blood-thirsty as it was cruel. It pushed itself right inside the town gate and devoured all the cattle it could find. It breathed fire so wherever it went things turned to ashes and crumbled down as dust. Trees died and flowers dried up and the grass turned to charcoal whenever the dragon appeared.

"Shut the gates" ordered the king. "Don't let the dreadful creature come in."

The gates were shut, but the dragon appeared and knocked against the wall which started shaking.

The people were shaking in fear too.

"Please do something. Don't let the dragon kill us" they begged the king.

"Go back to the lake" the king said to the dragon. "We will keep two sheep for you just outside the gate every day. You can eat those. But don't come inside our gates."

The dragon went away and slithered into the lake. But everyone knew that he would break the wall if he did not find food and kill the people inside.

The people lived in a nightmare ever since. They knew that their supply of animals would run out some day. What would they do then? And what would the dragon do? The dreaded moment arrived before long. There were no more animals left inside the gates to offer the dragon!

"We have to offer the dragon human beings" said the king sadly, "there is no help for it. It is the only way to survive."

"But whom should we sacrifice?" the people asked in fear.

"I must be absolutely fair" said the king. "We shall make out a list with the names of everyone in the kingdom and have a lottery each day. The name that comes up in the lottery will be the person to face the dragon. What do you say?"

"It is quite fair" said the people. "Under the circumstances, it's the only thing to do."

So the people were more terrorized than ever, living in constant fear of being the next victim. The dragon soon found that eating human beings was even better than eating animals. So it started appearing earlier and earlier each day, almost before it was dawn. Then one day something terrible happened. The day's lottery brought up the name of Princess Sabra.

"How could you allow them to include her name in the list?" cried the Queen. "She is a princess, the princess of this land! I can't let her die."

"I had to include every name" said the king in a sad voice, 'Both yours and mine are there too. Perhaps I could go instead of Sabra."

"No, father" said Sabra in a firm voice. "I shall face the dragon tomorrow since my name has come up. We have to be fair to our people."

"Yes, my child" said the king wiping his tears, "Oh, if only the dragon had never come! How happy we all were before it arrived to wreck our happiness."

"And if only someone was brave and strong enough to kill it!" said Sabra.

"It's no use wishing for the impossible" said the Queen trying not to break down.

The next morning, Sabra was up before dawn. She wore the white wedding dress her mother had made for her since it was to be the last day of her life. She shuddered as she thought of the dragon. She had seen it from her window one morning. It looked so horrible and frightening that she had closed her window and had kept it closed ever since so that she might never see it again. And now she would have to be devoured by the monster. The Queen and the king embraced her tenderly before leading her outside the gate where the flag of their country fluttered in the air. Sabra stood under the flag waiting for the dragon to arrive. The king and the Queen left her there because they did not dare to keep the gate open.

Before long the hushed silence was broken and Sabra could hear the dragon gliding out of the water and the sound of crumbling grass which were charred. She could also hear something else. It sounded like someone riding a horse. Who could it be? As Sabra turned her faces she saw a white horse and a handsome knight carrying a blazing sword and shield. There was a loud hissing sound from the lakeside as the dragon was almost upon her. But, someone else reached her first. The brave knight hit the dragon with his sword that flashed like lightning. The dragon toppled for a moment.

"Quick! Give me your girdle" cried the knight.

Sabra tore off the white sash from her dress and gave it to the knight. The knight deftly looped it around the dragon's neck.

In the mean time, the people opened the gate and came out to see what had happened. The brave knight dragged the dragon right up to the market place and cut off its head with his sword.

How the people cheered! They went completely mad with joy and relief.

"Who are you, brave knight?" asked Sabra in wonder, How could you kill it?"

"I am George" said the knight, "I could kill it because I had the name of Christ on my lips. The dragon represented Evil and Evil can never exist where there is true faith."

"Bravo, young man" said the king. "Live with us and wed my daughter. You shall be our next king"

But George smiled and shook his head. "I am on a crusade" he said, "This is not my destination. But I wish Princess Sabra all happiness. I shall remember her in my prayers."

"Then share your faith with us" said the king, "the faith that gives one courage to face evil bravely and conquer it too."

"Gladly" said George and shared with all of them the message of Christianity.

As he rode away on his white horse, once again the people saw his white flag fluttering in the breeze. They could also see the emblem on the flag. It was a bright, single cross in red.

# The Lake that Saved a Love

*(A story from Scotland)*

Once upon a time there was a beautiful girl named Katherine. She lived by the lake Katrine, an important lake in Scotland. George Macduff, a charming young man, lived on the other side of the lake, in a village called Stronachlachar.

George fished in the lake and hunted in the forest nearby. He had a farm where he grew vegetables and a snug, warm little cottage where he lived. George was an excellent piper and often rowed over to the other side of the lake to play at weddings or other celebrations. During one such celebration he met Katherine. He was playing the *Eightsome Reel* , a popular Scottish folkdance, and saw her dancing, her face aglow with happiness. She was the most beautiful maiden he had ever come across.

George had never thought of marriage before. The very idea of settling down for life did not appeal to him. But he fell in love with Katherine on sight and made up his mind to marry her. Katherine's parents were dead so she lived with her aunt. He went to meet her there and felt that she was all that he had imagined her to be. Katherine also fell in love with him and the two were soon engaged to be married. Katherine gave him a locket with the picture of Saint Katherine, after whom she was named, as a token of her love.

"Keep it with you always. The blessed Saint Katherine will take care of you and protect you from all harm" Katherine said to George. She was a devout and pious girl with great faith in God and the saints.

"Do you really believe all this?" asked George, a little amused.

"Of course I do. With all my heart" answered Katherine. "All the more, because Saint Katherine is also the patron saint of Lake Katrine and I love the lake."

"Well, then, I shall keep it with me to please you" said George.

"Do you promise that?"

George promised and Katherine believed him.

Unfortunately, George was quite different from Katherine and did not share her simple faith. He did not believe in God or the saints. Nor did he ever go to church or say his prayers. If ever he mentioned God, it was in a tone of utter disrespect and ridicule. His father had been a disbeliever and George grew up to be like him. Although Katherine did not know his true nature, her aunt suspected it and felt that something was very wrong with his upbringing. But he was always so charming that she could not say anything. But she was not at all happy about the prospective wedding. She was also afraid that George was after Katherine's wealth rather than herself. Katherine's aunt had heard rumours about how George felt about church and God. She told Katherine that she should ask him to come to church with her to attend the special Christmas Eve service that evening.

But when Katherine asked him, George looked uncomfortable and tried to get out of it.

"I shall gladly escort you to the church but I shall not go in" said George.

"Why not?" asked Katherine surprised.

"I'm not the praying kind and most likely I shall be bored" said George.

"Bored! Inside a church? How can you?" said Katherine bewildered. "And the service will be beautiful this evening because it is Christmas Eve."

"Rest assured, I shall wait for you outside and bring you back home."

Katherine was so hurt at his decision and looked so unhappy that George finally gave in and said that he would attend the service with her.

Having made up his mind he brushed his best clothes and polished his shoes when there was a knock at his door. George was surprised because he thought everybody would be at the church already. And it was snowing outside. When he opened the door he, found a man in black who asked for shelter until it stopped snowing. George called him in and made him welcome. He found him a seat by the fire and gave him a drink to warm himself. But he was surprised to see that although it was snowing outside, the clothes and the boots of the stranger were remarkably clean and totally dry. He was even more surprised when he learned who the stranger was!

"I am the Devil" announced the stranger. "You are just the kind of man I need. That's why I have been looking for you"

"What do you mean?" asked George surprised.

"Well, you don't believe in God or the saints or the church. If you swear to be faithful to me I shall give you all the wealth you long for, and all the power you need."

"Indeed?" George could hardly believe his ears.

"Yes, for the rest of your life" said the Devil. "But in return you must swear never to utter the name of God again or ever enter a church."

George might have agreed at any other time. But now, as he thought of Katherine's trusting eyes, love won over greed and he told the devil that he could not do it. The devil was greatly annoyed and tried to tell him over and over again how wonderful it would be to have everything he wished for.

"You are being extremely foolish" he told him. "You will repent bitterly if you do not agree. After all, such a chance may never come again"

"I don't want your riches" said George firmly, "I shall not change my mind."

Finally the Devil left in a huff. He was so angry and disappointed that he sunk George's boat as he went out.

When George came out to row across the lake, he found that he had no boat to cross over to the other side! The church bells were already ringing, calling people to the service. If he tried to walk he could never make it in time. Then in a flash he remembered the locket. He took it out and addressed the patron saint of the lake. "Please, Saint Katherine, please let me reach the church in time" he prayed from the bottom of his heart, with all the sincerity that he was capable of. As he prayed, he noticed an extraordinary thing happen to the water of Lake Katrine. The water started freezing and made a pathway right across the lake. George stepped on it and slid over to the other side where Katherine stood waiting for him. The bells were still ringing when Katherine and George entered the church together. As they knelt side by side praying for their future happiness, the ice melted once again and there was no trace of the frozen path that had brought George across the lake. According to local legends, that was the only time that the lake Katrine ever froze!

# The Enchanted Bottle

*(A story from Ireland)*

Long, long ago there was a farmer named Mick Purcell who lived near the city of Cork. His wife was called Molly. Mick was very, very poor. Most of his land was barren and all he had was a small patch of potatoes and another of oats. And the land was merely rented because it was of no use to his landlord and he did not want it. Mick also had a cow, a pig and a few hens. Mick's children were too young to help him. Molly milked the cow and fed the children on boiled potatoes. The only money they managed to make was by selling the few eggs and most of the milk at Mallow, the nearest market.

It was a very hard life. But Mick and Molly did not complain and always hoped for better things. Then there came a particularly bad year. All their oats were spoiled. The hen and all the chickens died of some disease. Even the pig looked sick.

"What shall we do, Molly?" asked Mick in despair, "How shall we feed the children and keep a roof over our head? And pay rent to the landlord?"

"Sell the pig at Mallow" said Molly, "We can't sell our cow. It's the only thing we have."

But the pig fetched very little money. So little that it was spent before they could even count it!

"What shall we do now?" asked Mick

"We have no choice, Mick. You just have to go to Cork tomorrow and sell our cow" said Molly, "Luckily she is a good one and you should be able to sell her at a good price."

"But what shall we do once she is gone?" asked Mick looking at the children, "How will you feed them if we don't even have the milk to sell?"

"I expect God will look after us and help us manage somehow" said Molly.

"You are right" said Mick cheering up, "I shall not worry any more."

The next morning, as Mick prepared to go to Cork with the cow Molly said, "Don't sell her to the first person you come across. See who offers the highest price and sell her to him. After all, we do need the money badly."

"I'll remember" promised Mick and set off on his long 13-mile journey. As he crossed the stream surrounding the old abbey of Mourne he said to himself, "If only I had some money and didn't have to sell my cow!" Then he told himself that perhaps God would help him find the money he needed so badly.

It was a fine day and the sun shone brightly overhead. He crossed a long stretch of hilly region and after six long miles came to the top of a hill. Just then a tiny little man overtook him, saying "Good morning to you."

"Good morning" said Mick looking at the man curiously. He looked more like a dwarf and had a wrinkled, yellow face rather like a dried cauliflower. His hair was snow white and he had a sharp nose and red eyes that seemed to take in everything at a glance. Mick shivered. He did not like the look of the little man. What was even more strange was the fact that he was wearing a big coat that reached his feet although it was a bright and sunny day and quite warm. Mick walked faster as he drove the cow. But the little man kept pace with him very easily. In fact Mick found it impossible to walk ahead of him, although he was so much taller and took big strides. The dwarf seemed to glide beside him like a shadow. Mick shivered. If only the he hadn't been driving the cow he could have run away. The little man made him feel so uncomfortable!

"Well, where are you taking the cow, Mick Purcell?" asked the little man.

Mick jumped. "How did you know my name?" he asked.

"Never mind that. Tell me where are you taking her."

"To the cattle fair in Cork" answered Mick, not knowing what else to do.

"Are you planning to sell her?"

"Yes."

"Well then, sell her to me" said the little man.

Mick did not want to sell her cow to this strange little man. But he was afraid to say 'no'.

"What will you give me for her?" he asked.

"I'll give you this bottle" he said, pulling out an empty bottle from his pocket.

Mick could not help laughing. "Do you take me for a fool? Of course I won't give her for an empty bottle. What an idea!"

"You will be a fool if you refuse, because this bottle is worth far more than any money you may get at Cork" said the little man, "I tell you, you will not be sorry if you listen to me."

"But what shall I tell my wife? And how shall I feed my children? She will think me totally mad!" said Mick.

"I'm giving you the offer for the last time, Mick Purcell" said the little man shaking his head, "Take it or leave it."

"But what shall I do with an empty bottle?" he asked.

"I shall tell you what you should do" said the little man. "When you reach home ask your wife Molly to sweep the room clean and put a clean tablecloth on the table. Then place the bottle on the table and say, "bottle, do your duty".

"It sounds crazy" said Mick.

"If you listen to my words all your problems will vanish and you will be a rich man. But, if you refuse my offer you will beg for the rest of your life. Choose what you will do because I shall not wait any more" said the little man.

Mick did not dare to refuse him. He gave his cow to the little man and took the bottle from him. "If you are playing a trick on me the curse of a poor family will be on you" he told the old man.

"Good bye, Mick Purcell. You will be a rich man soon" said the little man and vanished right before his eyes.

"Good God!" cried Mick astonished, "was he one of the little men belonging to fairy folk? I didn't think they existed any more!" he put the bottle in his pocket carefully. He mustn't break it, whatever happened!

Molly was very angry when she found that Mick had brought home no money. But she grew quiet when she heard about the little man and swept the house clean. Then she took out the one and only clean tablecloth she possessed and spread it on the table. Mick put the bottle on the table and said, "Bottle do your duty". And immediately a strange thing happened. Two tiny little creatures stepped out of the bottle and covered the whole table with big gold and silver plates full of the most delicious food they had ever seen. It was far more than even a hungry family like theirs could eat. But they did enjoy the delicious meal, the best they had ever had in their lives.

"Will the little creatures take away all these lovely plates, mammy?" asked the children.

"I don't know. Let us wait and see" said Mick.

But the little people did not come out of the bottle again and the plates remained where they were. Molly washed and put them away carefully.

"Your little man was right, Mick. We shall be very rich if we get plates like these for every meal" she said happily.

Mick sold the gold and silver plates in Cork and got a lot of money for them. Before long he bought a lot of land and cattle and had a fine, big farm and everything they had ever wanted. But Mick's previous landlord got to hear of it and came and asked him how he made so much money. He gave him no peace until Mick told him about the bottle. The landlord simply snatched the bottle away and left the place.

"Let him have it" said Mick, "We have enough money."

But another bad year came soon after and there were no crops and the cattle died. And Mick had no more money. They became as poor as before with nothing left except a cow. Mick decided to go to Cork again to sell the cow, hoping he would come across the little man once more and ask him for another bottle. It was a bright and sunny day when he had gone the last time. Today it was cloudy and misty and Mick could hardly see his way. But the same little man overtook him once again.

"Well, Mick Purcell, are you a rich man now?"

"I was, good sir, but I have lost all my money now. If only you can give me another bottle you can have this cow. It's the only thing I have."

"Very well. I shall give you another" said the little man handing him another bottle like the first one, "I shall take this cow instead."

"Thank you, good sir" cried Mick and rushed home with the bottle.

Mick asked Molly to sweep the house and lay a clean cloth on the table like the last time. Then he placed the new bottle on the table and said, 'bottle, do your duty".

But this time two big and hefty men climbed out of the bottle with big, strong sticks in their hands and beat up Mick, Molly and the children until they lay on the floor half dead.

"What a shabby trick to play!" cried Molly. But Mick was deep in thought.

"I think I understand" he said and went out of the room carrying the bottle with him.

He went straight to his previous landlord's house. The landlord was now rolling in money and had built a huge palace. At first he refused to see a poor man like Mick. But when Mick sent word that he had another bottle like the first one and that he had come to show it to him, the landlord came running.

"I hear you have another bottle?" said the landlord, "Where is it?"

"I shall show you when you take me to your hall and spread a fresh tablecloth on your table" said Mick.

"Ah yes, I remember" said the landlord and took him to the hall where all his new friends were having a feast.

Mick placed the bottle on the table and said, "Bottle, do your duty". He had already seen his first bottle on the shelf. Instantly the two stout men came out and bashed up everyone in the hall especially the landlord.

"Stop these two devils from hurting us" cried the landlord, "or I shall kill you myself"

"Not until you have given me back my first bottle which I see on this shelf" said Mick, "You had taken it from me by force."

"I shall NOT give it back" screamed the landlord.

"Then I shall not call off these two creatures" said Mick, "Have it your own way."

But the other people were screaming their heads off.

"We shall all be dead if these two go on" they told the landlord, "for goodness' sake let Mick have his bottle back. Or else you too shall be dead like the rest of us."

At last the landlord felt that enough was enough and he told Mick he might have his bottle back, provided he got the two men off their backs.

Mick picked up his bottle from the shelf. Immediately the two men shrunk in size and got into the bottle. Mick carried them home with him. The old bottle soon gave him all the gold plates he wanted and Mick grew rich and prosperous once again. He lived happily with his wife Molly and the children and never had any more problems in his life. You might wonder what happened to the magic bottle. Well, the servants tried to steal it but while they were passing it from one hand to another, it fell down and broke into pieces.

So no one was able to use it ever again!

# Betty and Her Baby

*(A story from Wales)*

Betty Stoggs sat in the sun peeling apples. It was a special day for her.

Betty was 17 years old today and her parents wanted her to select her husband from among her various suitors. Betty was not sure which of them she liked best. So she chose the old-fashioned way of finding out. After peeling all the apples she walked under the apple tree, closed her eyes and threw the peels over her right shoulder, chanting the ancient rhyme:

*"Apple tree, apple tree*

*Show my true love's name to me"*

When Betty opened her eyes she found that the peels had fallen on the ground forming the letter "J". it meant that the man she would marry would have a name that started with a "J". Betty frowned and tried to remember all the farmers that she knew whose name started with that letter.

Jacky of Lelant? Oh no, he was too old!

John? But he was already engaged to Nan!

What about Jim and Josiah? Well, both were too young for her!

Well, Jan the miner then? He was not too old. Nor was he married or engaged to anyone. Besides, he was a good man and also good looking. Yes, Jan was the right man for her!

Betty Stoggs was a pretty girl. Very shortly Jan, the miner came and they were married.

Betty left for her new home with her husband. Jan was down at the mines all day while Betty remained at home with Jan's old mother. Now, Jan's mother did not like Betty at all and made life quite miserable for her. She made Betty work from dawn to dusk – making her cook and sew and knit and run a hundred errands all day long until Betty was both wild and miserable. So when Jan returned home after work, Betty just cried and cried.

"What is it, Betty?" he asked her anxiously, "what is it you want? Tell me and I shall get it for you."

"I want my own home where I can live all by myself and do just as I want, with just you" said Betty.

"Very well, if that's what you wish for" said Jan.

From the very next day, Jan spent all his free time building a cottage for Betty. It was complete in a year's time and looked as pretty as a picture. Jan built it at the edge of a moor in a place that was called Towednack. Betty clapped her hands in joy when she saw it.

Betty and Jan soon moved into their new home. Betty sang and whistled all day long as she went about her work. She was so pleased to be able to do what she liked. But Betty was basically a lazy girl and hated work of any kind. As the days went by she got up from bed very late, did not bother to cook breakfast for Jan or pack him his lunch. In fact, on most days it was well past noon by the time she got up. But Jan did not complain. Betty seemed happy. And so was he.

But as the days passed Betty's new cottage grew dirty and grimy. There were cobwebs in every corner, grime on all the window panes and heaps of dust everywhere. The sunlight refused to come in and everywhere there was just dirt and disorder. Betty grew grumpy and sullen and quarreled with Jan.

"You are always enjoying yourself with the other fellows down at the mines" she told him, "But just look at me! All alone in this place which is as gloomy as a grave!"

"Well, it was good enough when it was clean" said Jan, "If you were to sweep and dust the place and mop up the windows, the sunlight would come in and it wouldn't look so gloomy....."

"Don't be stupid! I don't need to do any of those things. I hate it here because I have no company" said Betty.

"Very well. Let me see what I can do" said Jan.

That evening, when Jan returned home he brought a tabby cat for Betty. "Here, this cat will be company for you when I am away" he told her. Betty clapped her hands when she saw it and was happy. Jan felt happy too. He did not complain because Betty never cooked a decent meal for him, not even supper.

Betty was no longer lonely. The tabby cat went everywhere with her. It played with the dust balls in every corner and with her yarn when she knitted. It climbed up into Betty's lap and went to sleep. Somehow Betty never forgot to feed the cat. And since she cooked for the cat, she remembered to cook something for Jan as well. For a time all seemed well. Then one evening, Jan returned home to find the entire house in a big mess and no supper. Betty was crying loudly in one corner and the cat was howling in another.

"Good heavens! What is the matter?" cried Jan in alarm.

"We are lonely!" sobbed Betty, "My cat has no one to play with and I have no one to talk to."

"You have each other" said Jan, "Things have been fine so far."

"The cat can only mew and purr" said Betty.

"What more do you want?" asked Jan surprised.

Betty said nothing and just went on crying.

But Betty was happy when she had a baby the following year. A lovely big boy who laughed and crawled about the place. He was named Jan after his father but everyone called him "Wee Jan". Tabby also loved Wee Jan. The two of them slept in the same cradle and drank milk from the same bowl and played together in the dust. Very soon Wee Jan was as black as tabby because he was so thickly coated with dust and dirt. Jan often complained and asked Betty to wash and bathe Wee Jan, so that he wouldn't look so grimy. But as usual Betty was too lazy to listen to his words.

"It's good that Wee Jan is covered with soot" she said to Jan, "He won't feel the cold wind now. You know how cold our moor is."

Only tabby licked him clean sometimes when it washed its own face.

Wee John grew bigger as days passed. Sometimes he cried and fretted, either because he was hungry or because he was uncomfortable. Betty soon thought the baby a big bother and left him alone in the cottage with tabby, while she went to town and stayed there chatting with people and listening to gossip.

"Have you left your baby all alone in the cottage?" they asked Betty in surprise.

"It's only for a little while" said Betty, "Besides, tabby is there. Wee Jan loves to play with it."

Day after day Betty tucked Wee Jan in the cradle with tabby and went gossiping in town. One midsummer day, she stayed back longer than usual and twilight had set in by the time she returned to Towednack. Betty walked fast because she did not want Jan to return home before her and find out that she had left Wee Jan all alone all this time. Besides, she had not even cooked anything for supper.

When she reached home she found the door wide open. Was Jan home before her? But no, there was no trace of Jan. The entire place was topsy turvy and the cradle was empty. There was no Wee Jan and no tabby!

Good gracious! Where had they vanished? Betty started looking for her baby everywhere – in the dirty corners, among the dust heaps that covered the whole cottage, among the cobwebs that covered the entire ceiling. There were spiders and mice and fleas and worms. But no baby and no tabby either!

Betty sat down on the floor and cried. How she cried! Jan heard her crying from the mines. People across the moor heard her crying and came running to see what the matter was. They saw Betty tearing pieces from her apron to wipe her tears.

"My baby is gone! My Wee Jan is gone! Oh what shall I do?"

"Do?" cried Jan in a rage, "Betty Stoggs, you have got to find my baby or I shall leave you too. You neglected him all these days and never looked after him properly. You never looked after me or the house that I built you with so much love. You are selfish and lazy and unfeeling and you do not deserve the dear little baby or a husband either. You go and find him or you will find yourself all alone for the rest of your life."

Betty was scared now. She ran out into the moonlit moor to look for her lost baby. Jan and all the others also joined in the search. "My little Jan! my sweet little Wee Jan, come home to mammy" wept Betty. But all she heard was the hoot of an owl. They looked everywhere – in every nook and cranny, in every bush and bank, in every croft and hedge for miles and miles around. But, there was no trace of Wee Jan or tabby. At daybreak, the people returned to their own homes across the moor. Jan returned to his cottage in Towednack to have a quiet cry. Only Betty continued to look for her baby.

The next morning, Betty suddenly heard a tiny sound from under a gorse bush. Her heart leaped in joy because she knew that sound. She crawled under the bush, getting badly hurt by its thorns. But there under the bush lay tabby and beside him was Wee Jan fast asleep. But what a different Wee Jan. He was clean and well scrubbed and smelt like a flower. Under his little head was a pillow of rose petals. He was tightly wrapped and covered in a bright satin cloth. Betty gathered him into her arms and ran all the way to her cottage, tabby following close behind.

When Jan saw them he was wild with joy. He hugged and kissed Wee Jan who was still fast asleep. The neighbours came in and rejoiced with them. An old woman picked up Wee John and saw a small black mark of soot on his feet.

"See here, Betty, this is a mark made by the fairies" she said to Betty, "They had carried him away and were cleaning him up before taking him away to fairyland. But the sun rose before they could clean his feet and they had to fly back to fairyland leaving him behind. Look at this satin. Everyone knows how the fairies love it. They always steal it whenever they see any drying on the hedges."

"But I have Wee Jan safe now" said Betty.

"Yes, but the fairies will look for him everywhere" said the old woman, "they will carry him away again if they get a chance."

"But they will not get a chance" said Betty laughing. "Now that I have my baby back, I shall never, never leave him alone for a single moment."

Betty was as good as her word. She cleaned up the entire cottage until it shone and sparkled as it had done when it was new. She kept Wee Jan clean and well fed and also fed tabby too. She cut up the satin cloth and made shirts for Wee Jan. She cleaned the windows until the sunlight streamed in. Jan always found the place neat and clean and his meals were well cooked and piping hot.

Betty tried her best to clean the black mark from Wee Jan's feet. But the mark remained.

"It's a fairy mark" said the old woman.

"No, it's a lucky mark" said Betty, "The mark changed my whole life for the better. I now know that this happiness is going to last forever."

And it did!

# Helga's Friend

*(A story from Austria)*

Most of us are afraid of snakes. Especially those that are poisonous. But this story is about a snake and a girl named Helga and what happened when she was kind to the snake.

Helga was a poor little girl who was quite alone in the world.

She had no father or mother, no brother or sister. In fact she had no relative who would look after her or give her shelter. So she found work with a farmer after her parents died because she had to make a living. The farmer and his wife did not pay her any wages and made her work very hard. But at least they gave her three square meals a day and a bed to sleep on. Helga did not complain and was grateful for what they gave her.

It was the farmer's wife who always milked the cows. But one morning it was snowing hard and it was bitterly cold outside. The farmer's wife woke Helga up and said,

'Helga, Helga, go and milk the cows'. The cowshed was far away. Helga was wet and shivering by the time she reached the shed. She started milking the cows, her hands almost freezing in the cold. As soon as her bucket was full, she heard a hissing sound behind. Turning back she saw a huge adder sliding towards her. It had a little golden crown on its head. Helga wanted to scream but stopped when she looked at the adder's eyes. It had such a thirsty look that she felt sorry and lowered her bucket. The adder lapped up the milk

and gave her a grateful look. Then it turned back and slipped away outside the shed.

Helga felt afraid when she saw that the adder had finished up all the milk and there was just a trickle left at the bottom of the bucket. She knew that the farmer's wife would beat her and not give her any breakfast at all. She crept inside the house shaking in fear.

'Helga, Helga, have you milked the cows?' asked the farmer's wife from the kitchen.

'Yes' replied Helga wondering what would happen next.

'Bring the bucket here and pour the milk inside the milk pan' said the farmer's wife.

Helga turned her bucket and lo and behold, milk simply gushed out of her bucket! In fact, there was so much milk that three huge milk pans brimmed over instead of just one.

'Clever girl!' said the farmer's wife smiling at her for the first time in her life, 'I shall send you to milk the cows every morning.'

'On no, please don't' said Helga remembering the adder, 'please give me something else to do.'

'You will milk the cows every day from now on – both morning and evening', said the farmer's wife firmly, 'or you shall go hungry. I have no food to waste on disobedient little girls!'

Helga said no more because she knew it was no use. She went to milk the cows every day and every day the adder came and drank up all the milk in her bucket. The milk overflowed every time she went back home and the farmer's wife got far more than what she expected. It put her in a very good mood for the rest of the day. She stopped being unkind to Helga and gave her proper meals. She did wonder, of course, why the cows gave so much more milk whenever Helga went to milk them. But fortunately, she did not go to check it out herself! So no one got to know about the adder. Helga was no longer afraid of the adder. In fact she got very fond of it because it made life so much easier for her. She only wished it could speak to her. But though the adder could not speak, it always gave her a look of trust and gratitude which made Helga very happy.

Years flew by. Helga was now a young woman and a very beautiful one. She was courted by many young farmers who wanted to marry her. The farmer and his wife knew that Helga would not live with them for long because she would eventually choose one of them and have a home of her own. They were now quite kind to her. Helga continued to milk the cows and do all her usual chores. She was not sure which of the young farmers she wanted to marry and so she kept herself aloof. But one day, Helga fell in love with one of the young farmers because he seemed very different from all the rest and she knew in her heart that he was the right man for her. So, she promised to marry him when he asked her and was very happy. The wedding day was fixed up by the young farmer's family. The farmer and his wife also decided to hold a wedding feast for Helga. After all, she had served them faithfully all these years and never gave them any cause to doubt her loyalty.

Helga went to milk the cows for the last time. The adder came to drink the milk as usual.

'You know, dear adder, this is the last time I shall feed you' said Helga, 'Because I am getting married tomorrow. After the wedding I shall go away with my husband to my new home and not see you again. My husband does not own any cows, so I shall not be able to give you milk after this.'

The adder gave her a sorrowful look.

'I shall miss you, dear adder' said Helga, 'You have been so good to me. The farmer I am getting married to is a poor man and does not have many things in his house. But I don't mind. He is a good and kind man and I know that I shall be happy even if we are poor. Do wish me joy'. The adder gave her a fixed look and quietly glided away.

Helga's wedding feast was a grand success. Everyone in the village was there. They ate and drank and danced and made merry. Suddenly, there was a hush and everyone stood still wondering what was wrong. At first they merely heard a hissing sound. Then they saw an adder with a golden crown gliding inside the barn. It went right up to the bride, climbed up on her shoulder and shook its crown until it fell on her lap. Then it glided back quietly out into the darkness. Everybody was stunned. But Helga had tears in her eyes when she saw how her friend had come to attend her wedding feast. She picked up the little golden crown and kept it in her purse. The feast and merry making went on until the small hours of the morning. When Helga opened her purse the next morning, she found it full of gold! The moment she shook out the gold coins it got filled up with more gold coins. And it happened again and again, every time. From that night her purse was never empty no matter how much gold she took out and Helga and her husband became the richest people in the land. But they were loved by all not because they were rich, but because they were good and generous and gave things freely to the others, especially the farmers who had given Helga a home. They were the happiest couple in the land because they had been good enough to share their good fortune with those less fortunate. And they continued to live happily ever after.

# The Challenge

*(A story from Switzerland)*

There is a saying in German which describes a bad or a clumsy worker as one who is "as foolish as the devil who had to run round the house three times for every stitch". The story which led to this proverb is very interesting. It is said to have happened in Switzerland, one of the most beautiful countries in the world.

Once upon a time there lived a woman, Madame Cleo, who was very clever at sewing things. Those were the days when there were no sewing machines and everything had to be stitched by hand. Madame Cleo was in great demand because she could sew really fast. Whenever anyone wanted new clothes, they would rush to her and get her to do the sewing. With so much work at her disposal Madame Cleo soon grew to be a very rich woman, which was not bad. But as she became richer and richer she became prouder and prouder of her skill and began boasting about it to everyone. Now, this was not good at all and soon led to something unexpected.

"I have no equal so far as sewing goes" said Madame Cleo to everyone who came to her for work.

"Indeed that is true, madame" most of them would reply.

"I am cleverer than anyone who can wield a needle" she would continue, "I am sure I could beat the devil himself if it came to sewing!"

"You'd better not say it so loud" said her clients looking uncomfortable, "What if the devil were to hear you? I'm sure you would not like him to challenge you, whatever you may say."

"Oh, I'm not afraid of the devil. I know I am far cleverer than he is" said Madame Cleo.

But one day the devil was passing by Madame Cleo's house and actually heard her say these words. The devil was livid with anger. How dared this woman tell people that she was cleverer than the devil! Well, he would show her where such bragging led to.

The devil walked past her closed door and stood before her. "So you think you are more clever than I am, do you?" cried the devil, "Very well, I shall challenge you to a sewing race tomorrow. If you lose you will burn in hell forever. If you win, I shall never bother you again."

"I was only joking" said Madame Cleo shaking in fright. But the devil had already disappeared.

"We told you not to say such things" said her clients, "now see where your boasting has led you."

"I'll run away" said Madame Cleo, "the devil won't be able to find me."

"Don't be silly" said the people, "the devil will find you no matter where you hide. Just try to do your best, that's all. The devil may not be as clever as you, where sewing is concerned."

The devil turned up early the next morning and called out all the people who had been at Madame Cleo's place when the devil had challenged her. He wanted them to witness the sewing competition. In fact the news had already spread far and wide and every one in the land gathered to see the challenge between Madame Cleo and the devil. It was decided that they would each make a shirt and see who could finish it first.

The devil had brought two pieces of cloth, two pairs of scissors and two big reels of thread for the competition. The challenge began with the cutting out of the shirt.

Snap snap! went the scissors of the seamstress.

Snap snap! went the scissors of the devil.

But both took exactly the same time to cut out the shirt. Madame Cleo heaved a sigh of relief. The devil frowned.

But once they started sewing things took an unexpected turn. The devil had never made a shirt in his life before and had no idea how to go about it. More than anything else, he wanted to save time so that he could finish the shirt before Madame Cleo did. So he threaded the entire reel of cotton so that he might not have to waste any time re-threading his needle. But it was a very foolish thing to do. Because every time he made a stitch he had to run round the house three times to pull the thread through. Also, he made just one stitch at a time with his needle instead of making several. What's more, he quite forgot to tie a knot at the end of the thread. So after he had run round the house three times he discovered that the stitch had come out. So he had to do it all over again.

The devil tied a knot this time, but because he had to run after every stitch, he grew very tired after a while and began to huff and puff. Then something else happened. Because he had taken the entire reel at one go, the thread got tangled up with knots and the devil had to undo each one before he could make the next stitch. He muttered and cursed loudly but made no headway with the shirt at all.

But Madame Cleo was an expert at sewing and had made dozens of shirts every week. She threaded the needle with a convenient amount of thread and made a strong knot at the end so that the stitch would not come out. She went on and on sewing, steadily and quickly, and never once looked up until the shirt was complete. Once it was made, she raised her eyes to see what the devil was doing and whether he had already completed the shirt before her. But she could not see the devil or the shirt he was making. She wondered what had happened when she saw the devil coming round the house, huffing and puffing, the needle in his hand. The cloth lay on the ground with just a few stitches on it. The devil had not been able to complete even one full seam!

Madame Cleo was delighted and threw the shirt at the devil. The devil was so ashamed to be beaten by a mere woman that he sank into the ground in a glow of flames and never returned again. In fact, he never dared to accept another sewing challenge. And Madame

Cleo had also learned her lesson. She never said a single word about her cleverness after that. She realized what a narrow escape she had! But the story of her having a competition with the devil was remembered by all. So, even now, when a person does any work in a clumsy manner, people say that he is as foolish as the devil who had to run round the house three times for every stitch"!

# How River Ganga Came Down to the Earth

*(A Story from India)*

All of you must know that the Ganga is the most important river in India. It is also a sacred river which was once said to be located in heaven. This is the story of how and why it came down to the earth.

Long ago, there lived a mighty king named Sagar in the kingdom of Ayodhya. He had two Queens. The elder Queen had just one son who was called Asamanja. The younger Queen had sixty thousand sons! King Sagar was childless for very many years. He was greatly worried and very unhappy, wondering who would look after his kingdom after him. One day, he trudged up the Kailasa mountains which was the abode of Lord Siva, taking both his Queens with him. All three prayed earnestly day and night that the Lord might bless them with children.

Lord Siva was moved by the sincerity of their prayers and gave them his blessings. Very soon, the Queens realized that their prayer was to be fulfilled. But, while a bonny son was born to the elder Queen, the second Queen gave birth to an object that looked like a gourd! Bitterly disappointed, she was about to throw it away, when she heard a voice commanding her to preserve it. The gourd contained sixty thousand little seeds. In a short while, each of the seeds turned into a little prince!

After many years of reign, King Sagar decided to perform the Ashwamedha yajna. This was a ritual attempted by only the most powerful of kings. It was done by letting loose a splendid white horse which would roam freely all over the kingdom. Whoever captured the horse had to fight the warrior guarding the horse and defeat him. If the horse returned unchallenged by anyone, it meant that the king had been accepted and acknowledged as the supreme ruler by all. It was the greatest honour a king could have.

The news that King Sagar was about to perform the Ashwamedha spread far and wide. Indra the king of heaven also got to hear about it. When Indra realized that the horse would be guarded by sixty thousand and one sons of king Sagar, he grew very nervous. How could any king be a match against so many? And yet, if Indra failed to capture the horse, Sagar would become the king of heaven instead of him. He couldn't even bear to think about it! Only a trick could save the situation. Indra thought and thought and finally hit upon an idea. He made himself invisible and quietly stole the horse one night and led it to the seashore where sage Kapila had his hermitage. He tied the horse to a tree within the hermitage and left the place smiling triumphantly. "Well, well, King Sagar, now you just wait and see what happens! No Ashwamedha yajna for you, that's certain!" he told himself in glee. In the mean time, every one in Sagar's kingdom grew frantic at the sudden disappearance of the yajna horse.

Sixty thousand sons of the younger Queen set off at once, determined to find it. They finally discovered the horse tied to a tree inside Kapila's hermitage.

"Just look at that!" cried the eldest of the sixty thousand.

"Stealing our horse and keeping it tied up!" cried another.

"And he dares to call himself a sage!" cried all the rest.

Sage Kapila who was in deep meditation at the time knew nothing about the horse. But the rude and angry shouting of the princes made him open his eyes. Furious at being disturbed while in prayers, he looked at them. And the fire that shot out of his angry eyes reduced all sixty thousand princes to ashes.

When the news reached king Sagar, he was prostrate with grief. Little Angshuman, king Sagar's grandson (son of his eldest son

Asamanja), found his way to sage Kapila's hermitage and begged him to return his grandfather's horse so that he might perform the yajna.

"I didn't bring it, son" said the sage, "I have no idea how it came here. But take it by all means."

"And sir, please bring my sixty thousand uncles back to life."

"I am afraid I can't do that" said sage Kapila, "you see, they were not destined to live any longer."

"Then tell me what I should do to make them live again" cried the little boy.

"Nothing can be done right now" said the sage, shaking his head, "but a boy named Bhagirath will be born in your family years later and he will bring them back to life."

"And how will he do that?" asked Angshuman .

"He will bring down Ganges, the river of heaven, on earth. When its water touches the ashes of your uncles, they will come back to life."

"If she is a river why can't she just flow down here? Why does she need someone to bring her down?"

"Because she is now locked up in the worshipping bowl of Lord Brahma. Don't ask me why! It is too long a story." said sage Kapila, "but Lord Brahma will certainly release her when Bhagirath asks him to."

Angshuman returned to his grandfather with the horse. Sagar then performed the Ashwamedha yajna and was acknowledged the supreme ruler of the world.

Years later, when Bhagirath was born and was old enough to be told the story he renounced his kingdom and made for the Himalayas. There he prayed to Lord Brahma and he let the Ganges out of his worshipping bowl. Once released, the Ganges crashed down below with such force that the whole earth shook and trembled. She would have probably swept off every living creature from the face of the earth, had Lord Siva not intervened and held her captive in the matted locks of his hair! So the Ganges was imprisoned once again and once again Bhagirath had to pray to Lord Siva to set her free.

Finally, Lord Siva allowed the Ganges to fall on earth once again. But this time she fell in a mild seven-fold torrent. The wildest among the seven torrents followed Bhagirath as he walked. Bhagirath blew a conch shell all the way to let the people know that he was now escorting the Ganges to his own homeland. The Ganges rippled along joyfully over hills and dales. But Bhagirath's adventures were not yet over. Somewhere along the way the river passed the hermitage of sage Janhu. Janhu was deep in meditation when the gushing torrent of the Ganges swept away his prayer vessels. The sage was so angry that he drank up the entire river in a single gulp until there was not even a drop to be seen! Poor Bhagirath went down on his knees once again, begging sage Janhu to set the Ganges free. At last Janhu forgave the Ganges and let her out through his ears. At that point her name changed to **'Janhavi'** which means "daughter of Janhu", as it was like a new birth for her. People who live there still call the Ganges by that name.

Finally, Bhagirath brought the Ganges to the hermitage of sage Kapila, where the ashes of his forefathers lay in a heap. The Ganges rippled over the ashes and all sixty thousand sons of Sagar came to life once again. Her mission fulfilled, the Ganges now rushed into the sea. The place where all this happened is now known as "Ganga Sagar". It has been an important place for pilgrimage ever since. In Eastern India the Ganges is known as **"Bhagirathi"** in memory of King Bhagirath who had brought the river down on earth.

# There is no king as God

*(A story from Africa)*

Long ago in Nigeria, in West Africa, lived a king. His name was Yaburo. He was a mighty king, whose empire stretched far and wide. He commanded a great deal of respect from his people for he was both intelligent and powerful.

He held a large court three days a week. His people were welcome to speak about their problems or share their experiences. Everyone who came to his court would say, "May the king live forever" as the traditional greeting. Did I say everyone? Oops, I am sorry, I forgot about Olango. He earned his living as a teacher. Whenever he appeared before the king, he would say, "No King as God".

The mighty Yaburo did not like this but tolerated Olango since he did not want to appear cruel and unjust. But, gradually even his courtiers started whispering about him. Yaburo realised if something was not done quickly, people would stop treating him with the respect and awe he had always been used to.

After a lot of thinking, Yaburo thought of a plan which would enable him to eliminate Olango without any blame coming to him.

Yaburo called Olango to his court.

"Olango, I am giving you something which is very special to me to keep. I have chosen you since I trust you more than anyone else. You keep it very carefully and return it to me when I ask," - with these words, Yaburo handed over a silver ring to Olango, who took the ring without suspecting anything.

Olango went home and kept the ring in a dried and empty ram's horn and gave it to his wife Baiti.

"Keep this in a safe place and tell no one about it," he said.

Ten days later Yaburo called Olango to his court.

"Go to Dinidishu village which is to the extreme north of our kingdom. Go tell the people there that they have to come here immediately. We need their help in building the walls of our city."

As soon as Olango had left, Yaburo sent for Baiti.

"I know your husband has given you something for safekeeping. I want you to hand it over to me."

Baiti shook her head.

"I'll give you a million cowries," declared the King.

Cowries are small sea-shells which were used as currency as well as ornaments by the people of Africa in those days.

Baiti was tempted by the King's offer but she hesitated.

"My husband won't spare me when he comes to know," she said.

"And do you think I'll spare you, if you refuse me, your King. You and your entire family will suffer if you don't obey me," Yaburo thundered.

Terrified Baiti went home and returned with the horn.

The King looked into the horn and found the ring inside. He sent Baiti off with the million cowries. After she had left, he replaced the ring into the horn and asked his guards to throw it far into the biggest lake in Nigeria which never dried up. The guards obeyed his command and returned to the court.

As soon as the horn fell into the lake, a big fish swallowed it up.

A few days later, Olango was returning home. When he met some friends who were going fishing and joined them. He caught a big fish and went home, happy with his catch. As he was cleaning the fish, his knife struck something hard. It was the ram's horn. He pulled it out and on checking found the silver ring, which the king had given him, inside it.

"Truly," he said, "There is no king as God."

Just then, a royal messenger came to his house and told him, he was wanted by King Yaburo in his court immediately.

"Where is the ram's horn which I had given you," Olango asked his wife.

Baiti went around acting as if she was looking for it and then finally said, "I am sorry but I can't find it. I think the rats must have eaten it up."

Olango did not say anything. He was now able to gauge the King's plan. He was quite certain that the King had either tricked or forced Baiti to give the horn.

Olango set off for the royal court. When he reached there he found Yaburo hadn't come. A few minutes later Yaburo entered. All the courtiers jumped to their feet and declared, "May the King live forever."

But Olango quietly said, "There is no King as God."

The King advanced towards Olango and staring straight into his eyes asked, "Is it really true that there is no King as God?"

Olango firmly replied, "Yes."

"Okay, now give me the silver ring which I gave you," Yaburo said his eyes blazing. He was sure he had Olango cornered. Olango would not be able to produce the silver ring and would be promptly beheaded. And that would end all this 'no king as God' nonsense forever. He asked his guards to surround Olango.

However, King Yaburo was in for a rude shock. Olango calmly put his hands inside his robe and removing the horn gave it to the King. Yaburo upturned the horn and soon the silver ring was quietly nestling in his palm. The King stared at Olango in amazement for a few seconds, then slowly he said, "Yes, indeed there is no king like God." All his courtiers clapped in approval.

Later, Yaburo divided his kingdom into two. One half he kept with himself and the other he gave it to Olango to rule.

Both Yaburo and Olango ruled their respective kingdoms for long with faith in God.

# The Foolish Old Man of the North Mountain

*(A story from China)*

This is the tale of a very old man. He lived behind the Taihang and Wangwu mountains. These mountains were hundred thousand feet high and covered a distance of several hundred li (Chinese unit of length).

The man was called, the Foolish Old Man of the North Mountains. He was a happy and contented man of simple needs with only one grouse. One day, he called the members of his large family and addressed them, "Whenever we go south, the Taihang and Wangwu mountains block our way. We have to go around them. For all of us this is tedious but, for a man of my age and health this can be both tiring and tiresome."

Everyone nodded for they knew the old man was telling the truth.

"I have an idea. Why don't all of us work hard to level the two mountains. This way there will be a direct route from our home to the south", said the old man.

The old man's wife expressed her doubt, "You are old and feeble of strength. You will not be able to move even a small hill let alone tackle huge mountains like Taihang and Wangwu. Moreover, where will you deposit the earth and rocks?"

"They can be carried to the shores of the Bohai sea," suggested a few members of his family.

In the beginning, there were only two persons out there with the Old Man to help him in his great task – his son and grandson.

The three of them started breaking rocks and digging the earth. They carried the rubble in the baskets and dustbins to the shores of the Bohai sea and dumped it there. The seven year old son of a widow, one of the old man's neighbours, came to help them. It was back breaking work but, they toiled on. One trip to the sea took them a long time – they left in winter and came back in summer.

The Wise Old Man of the River Bend had been watching the old man and his team at work for quite sometime. He stopped the Old Man and said in a voice dripping with amusement, "How foolish you are old man ! At your age and with your failing health how can you even imagine removing these mountains. The very attempt at shifting so much earth and rock is laughable."

The old man heaved a long sigh and replied, "You are so arrogant that you cannot see reason. Even a widow and a child who have seen nothing of the world, as compared to you, seem wiser."

"What do you mean I can't see reason?" demanded the Wise Old Man, greatly annoyed at the Old Man's reply.

"I'll explain. When I die my work will be continued by my son and grandsons. And when they are no more, their sons and grandsons will work on the project. And so on and on, the task will be continued by my progeny till the mission is accomplished. But remember, though my progeny will keep growing, the mountains will not grow. Now, tell me why is it then not possible to level the great Taihang and Wangwu mountains?" said the old man.

The Wise Old Man of the River Bend just stood there stunned by the simple logic of the Old Man who had always been thought of as foolish.

The old man's words were heard by the God of Snakes. He rushed to the God of Heavens and told the entire story to his leader. The God of Heavens was moved by the determinations of the Old Man. He called two of his assistants and told them, "Shift Taihang and Wangwu mountains to either side so that a path is created between them."

The order was carried out and thus the Foolish Old Man of the North Mountain succeeded in the mission who everyone thought was impossible.

# Thor in the Land of the Giants

*(A story from Scandinavia)*

In the mythology of Scandinavia, Thor was the God of Thunder and the supreme creator. Named after the Germanic word for thunder he was a wild, red-haired and bearded figure who travelled across the sky in a chariot drawn by goats. Thor wielded a hammer, called Mjollnir, which represented a powerful thunderbolt. If thrown, the hammer would return to him like a boomerang.

Once Thor, accompanied by Loki, the trickster God and Thjalfi, his follower, set off on a long journey to giant land. At night they found a huge building with a wide opening along one side and decided to spend the night there.

After they had slept for a couple of hours, they were suddenly woken up by what seemed like an earthquake. The whole building was shaking. Terrified, the Gods took shelter in a small passage to the right of the building. While Thor stood guard with his hammer the other two took rest. A roaring sound could be heard at regular intervals outside all night long.

In the morning, they went out of the hall and found an enormous giant lying asleep and snoring away to glory.

"This giant's snores were causing all that deafening noise last night," Loki said looking in awe at the enormous creature.

"Don't you worry, I'll take care of him," Thor said buckling his belt. Just then with a huge grunt, which shook the building, the

giant woke up and looked at the Gods who appeared puny in comparison.

"My name is Skrymir which means big fellow. And who are you?"

Thor introduced himself and his fellow travellers.

Skrymir bent down and picked up what they had taken for a hall but now realised was his glove.

"I assume you are going to my country, the land of the giants?" asked Skrymir.

"Yes, in fact we are," Thor nodded, looking at him with suspicion.

"Well we can go together sharing our food and chatting along the way," Big Fellow said, putting the Gods' provisions in his own bag.

They started off but very soon the giant's great strides took him far ahead.

Finally, the Gods caught up with Skrymir after nightfall. They found him sitting under an oak tree.

"Well friends get my supper ready while I take a quick nap. A big fellow like me needs much more sleep than little guys like you," the giant said.

Thor tried to undo the string, which tied the giant's bag in which the food was kept. However, for all his fabled strength and energetic efforts he did not succeed. Thor lost his temper and hit the sleeping giant on the head with his hammer.

Skrymir opened his eyes and gently asked, "Has a leaf dropped on my head?"

That night the Gods went without food. They also could not sleep a wink thanks to 'Big Fellow's' thunderous snores.

Finally, Thor could not bear it any longer and struck Skrymir a second time.

The giant opened one eye and quietly inquired, "Did an acorn fall on me this time?"

At dawn, the frustrated Thor struck him a third time with so much strength that the hammer sank into the giant's forehead.

This time Skrymir sat up.

"What happened? Did a naughty bird drop something on my forehead?" he asked.

Obviously the Gods were in no state to answer. The giant then got up.

"Though I know you have thoroughly enjoyed my company, the time has come for us to part. Be careful when you reach Utgard. There are plenty of giants in Utgard who are far bigger and not as gentle as I am." With these words Skrymir strode off much to the relief of Thor and his men.

They managed to reach the land of the giants without any more misadventures.

The King Utgard Loki's reception was not very warm.

"I have heard that you Gods are famous for your strength, skill, intelligence and courage. Let us see you display these virtues for us."

Thor accepted the challenge very confident that he and his companions would put up a splendid show. Many competitions were held pitting the visitors against the giants. The Gods were hopelessly outstripped in each and every event.

Thjalfi was defeated in running and Loki in an eating contest. Thor himself, a champion drinker was given a huge horn. He was sure he could empty it in one go, but even after he had taken three droughts, it seemed to be almost as full as at the beginning.

"It is a pity you couldn't complete the very first task given to you. Anyway the next job should be pretty easy even for you. You see my grey cat lying on the floor. All you have to do is to lift it," Utgard Loki mockingly said, looking at Thor.

This seemed a laughable task and Thor was confident he could do it with his left hand. But when he tried the cat wouldn't budge. He then made an attempt with both hands – the result was the same. Finally, he exerted all his considerable might but could do no more than raise one of its paws off the ground.

Utgard Loki should his head in mock despair.

"Okay here is a final task for you. Surely you won't let yourself and your country down by failing!"

He clapped thrice and an old woman entered.

"You have to wrestle with this old lady," the King declared.

Thor tried his might but was unable to move her. Exhausted, as he stepped back, the old woman grabbed him and brought him down to his knees in a few seconds. The fight was stopped by Utgard Loki but by then Thor's humiliation was complete.

Later the visitors were lavishly entertained and next morning they took leave of Utgard Loki. Skrymir accompanied them. Once they were out of the gates he addressed them, "Let me now reveal to you a few secrets. Thor you are stronger than us giants. But your power and strength were overcome by our cunning."

"Your cunning? I don't understand."

"I'll explain. The bag, which you could not undo, was not fastened by strings but by iron bands. The blows, which you believed had struck me, were actually diverted by magic into a mountain. Now if you go and have a look at the mountain, you'll find three deep pits in it."

"What about the contests?" Loki asked.

"I am coming to that. Your opponent in the eating contest was Fire, which consumes all things as no living creature can do. Thjalfi's competitor in the race was Thought which travels faster than any living creature," Skrymir said as the Gods gaped at him. Then turning to Thor he continued, "Thor, your horn had its tip in the sea, so that it never could be drained. However, the amount of water you swallowed was really huge, much more than of any of us can ever do. You know it even caused the tide to ebb."

"What about the grey cat and the old woman?" Thor asked.

"The grey cat was none other than your arch enemy the World Serpent which lies wrapped around all the worlds of the universe. And the old lady was actually 'Old Age', which can overcome even the strongest.

"So it was magic not skill and strength which defeated us," thundered Thor

Before Skrymir could answer Loki interrupted.

"Now tell us who are you? Are you actually Skrymir or....."

"Your suspicion is right Loki. I am not Skrymir. In fact there is no Skrymir. I am none other than your host Utgard Loki the King of the giants."

Hearing this Thor raised his hammer to strike but by then Utgard Loki had vanished into thin air leaving the trio of Gods – very angry but also somewhat humbled.

# The Land of Eternal Youth

*(A story from Ireland)*

If there were a land of Eternal youth wouldn't it be the most popular destination in the world?

Though we, in the modern world, know there is no such thing. In Irish mythology, there are legends associated with the Land of Eternal Youth. The most popular of these legends concerns Oisin - a very popular hero in Irish mythology.

His story begins with his father, Finn MacCool. Finn was a great military leader, visionary and poet. At a young age he became the leader of the Fianna who were an elite band of brave and powerful warriors. Under his leadership the Fianna grew into a formidable force.

One day, Finn and his men of the Fianna went out hunting. When they were returning a beautiful fawn strayed across their path. They chased the fawn but she was very quick. Finally, all were left behind except for Finn's two hounds Bran and Skeolaing. They chased the fawn through the forest and down into a valley until she could not run any further. She sat down wearily as the two hounds approached her. But the hounds did not attack her, rather they played with her. When the hounds returned Finn was surprised to find the fawn following them.

The beautiful and delicate creature followed Finn home and he gave her shelter in his garden. Next morning Finn was surprised to find a beautiful young woman standing by his bed.

"My name is Sara. I am the granddaughter of Dagda – the Lord of Perfect Knowledge. I was transferred into a fawn by an evil wizard. Your generousity and kindness has transformed me once again into a human."

Finn married her and they lived happily together for many months. One day, Finn had to leave home on a campaign related to the Fianna. When he returned home a week later he found his beloved missing. He searched everywhere for Sara but couldn't find her.

Several years later, Finn was hunting with his two hounds in the forest. He came across a little boy who was wild in appearance and had a tuft of deer hair on his forehead.

Finn recognised the boy as his son. He took him home and named him Oisin or the little fawn.

Years passed by and the boy grew up to be a great warrior and a talented poet. One day, Oisin was hunting with his father Finn and the Fiana. Suddenly, they saw a beautiful lady approaching. She wore gorgeous clothes, a crown of gold and sat astride a snow white horse. Her hair was golden, her skin alabaster and her eyes were blue.

"I am Niamh, the daughter of the sea God Manannan Mac Tir. My father is the king of Tir Na'Nog, the Land of Eternal Youth. I am searching for Oisin about whom I have heard so much."

Oisin stepped forward. "I am Oisin, the son of Finn Mac Cool," he said.

Oisin and Niamh instantly fell in love with each other.

"I have come to take you to the 'Land of Eternal Youth," the lovely Niamh said, her voice enticing and her smile enchanting.

Oisin bid farewell to Finn and the Fianna and climbed on the white horse. As his father and his companion watched the lovely couple rode towards the horizon they slowly disappeared from sight.

The journey went on and on and soon Oisin found there was mist all around. Just then Niamh waved her hand. The mist cleared to reveal a magnificent palace.

Tir Na' Nog, Oisin found, was bewitchingly beautiful. Melodious music, colours of every hue, chirping of birds and frolicking of animals – made it an idyllic place no one would ever like to leave. Everywhere Oisin looked, he saw the freshness of youth and the warmth of love. Oisin spent a blissful period of three weeks with the charming Niamh. Then he started feeling homesick. He started yearning for his father, the Fianna and his beloved Ireland.

"I want to go home and meet my people. They must surely be worried about me. I'll come back as soon as possible," he told Niamh.

The beautiful fairy was loathe to see Oisin go but had to give in to his request.

"Take my white horse but remember one thing – on no account, under no circumstances should you get off the horse and set foot on the soil."

Oisin nodded and set off on his long journey. His destination was the hill of Allen in country Kuldare, where his father's abode was.

When he reached the top of the hill he was in for a brutal shock. There was no dwelling in sight. All he could see was a landscape full of long, thick and unkempt grass and weeds, dotted by tall trees standing like ominous giants.

Oisin travelled on, his mind numb. He came across an old and feeble man trying to carry a heavy load.

Oisin, being kind by nature, instinctively jumped down to help the old man. As his feet landed on the soil he turned into a frail, feeble, blind and withered man himself.

Oisin then realised that the time spent in Tir Na' Nog – the Land of Eternal Youth – which had seemed like three weeks had actually been three hundred years............!

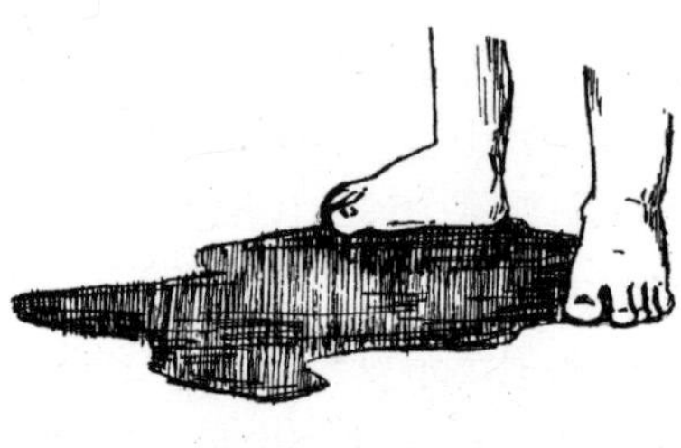

# The Divine Trinity

*(A story from Egypt)*

Osiris was the son of Nut, the Goddess of the sky and Geb, the earth. At the time of his birth a voice was heard in the temple: "Hear all you humans! The Lord of all has entered into light and the great and good king has been born."

When Osiris became king, he taught mankind how to worship Gods and drew up laws for them. Osiris ruled by the power of persuasion, not by force and was a popular and much revered king. He was helped in his administration by Thoth the moon God and Isis his faithful wife.

The chief enemy of Osiris was his own brother Set. He had red eyes and red hair and since red is considered to personify evil, Set was feared and hated. Set was very jealous of Osiris and there was a reason for that. Their father Geb had promised that his kingdom would be divided equally among his sons. The upper Egypt would be Set's and lower Egypt would go to Osiris. Set being greedy had claimed the whole kingdom as his. This had angered Geb and he had given the entire Egypt to Osiris. Burning with envy and hate, Set kept waiting for an opportunity to kill Osiris.

Once Osiris went on a long trip to spread the culture of Egypt far and wide. On his return Set invited him to a special banquet arranged in his honour. There he showed everyone a beautiful chest especially constructed to fit a king.

"I'll offer this chest to anyone who can lie down in it," Set declared.

Several guests tried but failed. Finally Osiris was invited. He got into the chest and lay down. Set quickly closed the lid and nailed it down. Set then had the chest weighed with lead and thrown into the flood waters of the river Nile.

When she heard the shocking news, Isis put on a widow's dress, cut off half her hair and weeping, set off to discover the body of her husband. She wandered to many lands asking everyone whether they had seen the chest. Finally she came across some children who told her they had seen it drifting towards the sea along the Tanitic branch of the Nile. Divine revelations informed her that the chest had been carried across the sea to Byblos in Phoenicia where it had been washed ashore at the foot of a tamarish tree. The tree had grown around the chest enclosing it completely. The king of Byblos, Malacander, admiring the great size of the tree had cut it down and used it as a pillar in his palace. Isis went to the King and pleaded with him. The kind King gave her the pillar. When the tamarish was cut it revealed the chest.

On her return to Egypt, Isis hid in the delta marshes in order to conceal from Set the discovery of the body. Set, however found the chest by a stroke of luck while hunting in the marshes at night. He recognised the body of his dead brother, tore it into 14 parts and scattered them throughout the kingdom.

Iris patiently began another search for her husband's body. She found the parts one by one and reconstructed the body. She then performed the rites of embalmment – a practice which later became sacred in Egypt. With the help of the many spells taught to her by Thoth, the Vizier of Osiris, Isis was able to restore her husband to eternal life.

After his resurrection, Osiris could have reclaimed his throne, but he preferred to maintain his kingdom in the land of the dead. As God of the dead, Osiris enjoyed his greatest popularity. He ultimately came to represent for his devotees the hope of an eternally happy life in another world ruled by a just and good king.

In the meanwhile, furious at the honours done to Osiris, Set seized Isis and threw her into a prison. Once again, Thoth came to her rescue and she managed to escape. She took refuge in a swamp where she gave birth to Horus – the son of Osiris.

Isis had no means to support herself except begging. One day, as usual she returned to the swamp and found Horus writhing in pain - half dead. Set, who was unable to enter the marshes in his real form, had taken the shape of a poisnous snake and bitten the infant.

Isis appealed to the Gods and Thoth descended in the boat of Ra the Sun God. When the boat stopped so did the light.

Thoth told Isis, "The power of Ra is at your disposal. The darkness will persist till Horus is cured. If Horus dies there will never again be light and the whole creation will be destroyed. If this happens, Set the symbol of evil will reign supreme. Hence, in the name of the Sun God Ra, I am removing the poison from the child's body and restoring him to life."

The powerful spell of the Sun God effectively cast by Thoth removed the poison and Horus was cured.

Horus, under the watchful eyes of his mother grew up to be a mighty warrior. He fought a fierce battle with Set slicing away vital parts of his body. Set too fought back. Taking the form of a pig, he tore out one of Horus' eyes. At this stage, the tribunal of the Gods intervened. Horus was awarded the entire kingdom and his torn eye was replaced. He, thus avenged the murder of his father - the brave Orisis and the torture of his mother - the beautiful Isis by the evil Set.

# The Great Land Master

*(A story from Japan)*

Long, long ago in Japan lived a hare called Oki. His place of dwelling was a tiny island off the Izumo peninsula.

Oki had only one ambition in life – to visit Izumo about which he had heard so much from his friends, the sea-gulls.

One day he approached Gimo the crocodile.

"Do you know Gimo there are more hare in our island than there are crocodiles in the sea?" Asked Oki.

"That is impossible. We are a large family we will definitely outnumber you," Gimo snorted.

"Okay then let us have a head count. All you crocodiles line up one after the other from here to Izumo. I'll hop on your backs one by one and count how many you are." Said Oki.

Gimo, who was a trifle slow witted, thought for sometime and agreed. He informed his family members about Oki's challenge.

The next day the crocodiles lined up from Oki's island to Izumo. Oki jumped on the back of Gimo and then landed on his brother. He continued moving from back to back at a brisk pace, loudly chanting the numbers.

Finally, he landed on the back of Mizo the smartest crocodile of the lot. Mizo, who was the last in the chain, guessed the motive of Oki and lashed out with his tail. Oki was sent flying and landed

on a heap on Izumo's beach. His white and soft fur was completely damaged.

At that point of time six brothers were proceeding towards the kingdom of Susamo – the mighty storm God. Their aim was to win the hand of his daughter, the beautiful Princess Inaba, in marriage.

As they were proceeding at a brisk pace, they found Oki lying in great pain on the sands.

"What is wrong with you?" asked the eldest brother.

Oki told the brothers his tale.

"That is what comes of being over smart," taunted the second brother.

"I have already been punished for my cunning. Now please help me or I'll die."

"We don't have time to waste over such silly things," the third brother said.

"Yes, if we delay further than none of us will get a chance to stake our claim for the hand of the princess," the fourth brother added.

"I have an idea," the fifth brother said and the hare looked up gratefully.

"You wash your fur in sea water and just lie down on the sea-shore. The wind will dry your fur and it will grow again."

"Great idea. When we come back with one of us having won the princess' hand we'll find you here bowing to us in gratitude," the sixth brother said barely managing to hide his smirk.

The brothers went on their way and poor Oki tried the remedy suggested by them. Naturally it had no effect, rather the pain only worsened.

As he was rolling on the beach in agony he saw a young man approaching him. He looked a bit like the others but was younger and better looking.

"Who are you and how did this happen to you?" asked the young man whose name was Yori, in a kind and gentle voice.

Oki told him the whole story including how the six men had taunted and tortured him.

"You must be talking about my brothers," Yori said and added, "But don't worry, I'll make sure you are fit and fine soon enough."

Yori bathed the hare in fresh water and dusted its skin with pollen. His touch was gentle and caring and white fur grew again in no time.

Yori told Oki that he too was going to woo the princess.

"Can I come along with you?" Oki asked.

"Why not?" Yori replied and the two friends set off together.

When they reached the palace Yori came to know his brothers had been rejected and had returned home.

Yori and Oki met the beautiful princess, Inaba. Yori fell in love with her at first glance and she too was charmed by the handsome young man. Oki told the princess about Yori's kindness and she was further impressed.

Yori and the Inaba were married. Yori became the ruler of Izumo and Oki lived happily with the couple.

In later years Yori became famous as a brave and just king and came to be known as the 'Great Land Master'.

# Vasilisa and Baba Yaga

*(A story from Russia)*

Vasilisa was a young girl with the loveliness of the moon and the radiance of the sun. She lived with her father and mother on the edge of a huge forest.

Once her mother fell ill and whatever Vasilisa and her father would do had no effect.

As she lay dying Vasilisa's mother gave her a cloth doll. "Vasilisa, this is a magic doll – Sveta. She will be your guide in future. Whenever you have a problem ask her and she will give you the right answer."

Vasilisa's mother died soon after. A year later her father remarried. His new wife had two ugly daughters of her own. All the three woman hated Vasilisa. Whenever her father went away on business, they would torment and torture her. Vasilisa would turn to Sveta who would invariably say, "Have patience, lovely Vasilisa. Everything will be okay."

One day, when her father was away Vasilisa's step mother called her. "There is no fire in the house. Go to Baba Yaga's hut in the forest and get a flame. Without fire we'll die of cold and hunger. I cannot go because I am too old and my daughters cannot go because they are too pretty. You are neither too old nor pretty – just the perfect person for this dangerous expedition. Go and come back before your father returns."

"Who is Baba Yaga?" Vasilisa asked Sveta when they were alone.

"Baba Yaga is an old and bony witch. Her teeth, nose and breasts are made of iron and her hair is a knot of writhing snakes. She lives deep in the forest in a house that sits on chicken legs – one in each corner so that it can move about," informed Sveta.

Vasilisa's lovely eyes grew round and the colour drained from her cheeks.

"W...will Baba Yaga eat me up?" Asked Vasilisa.

"People go to her for wisdom as well as many other things. She asks them questions and gives them tasks to perform. If they pass her tough 'tests' she grants them whatever they want or else ......"

"Or else...... she .......gobbles them up," Vasilisa completed the sentence her voice barely audible.

"Yes, that is true. But you don't worry, my dear Vasilisa, I am there with you," Sveta said and held out her little hand.

Vasilisa picked up Sveta and put her in her pocket and set off on her expedition.

Sveta guided her as Vaisilisa moved on, the thought of her father in her gentle heart and a prayer on her tender lips.

When Vasilisa arrived at Baba Yaga's house she stared in horror at the spectacle in front of her. The house was surrounded by a fence adorned with skulls that spew flames. Each hideous skill with its hollow eyes glaring at her looked straight out of her worst nightmare. The scene was so horrific that Vasilisa started trembling with fear. Just then an old and wrinkled witch flew out of the house and landed in front of the girl.

"Who are you? And what is it that you want?" the voice of Baba Yaga was soft and silky. Coming from a body so old and worn out the voice sounded even more eerie and hideous.

"M.....my name is Vasilisa. I ...I have come for fire Baba Yaga." Stammered Vasilisa.

"Why should I grant you your request?" demanded the witch.

Vasilisa was speechless for a few seconds. Sveta quietly whispered to her and Vasilisa repeated her words, "Because I ask for it, Baba Yaga."

"Yes, that was the answer I was looking for – short, simple and honest. Come inside the hut now. You will have to spend a week with me. I'll give you various tasks and if you perform them well, the fire is yours."

Vasilisa lived with Baba Yaga and with the help of Sveta completed all the tasks.

When the time came for Vasilisa to leave, Baba Yaga gave the girl a flaming skull.

Vasilisa took the skull, bid the witch goodbye and raced home. One the way she was surprised to find that the skull was actually a talking spirit who was gentle and kind.

When she reached home her stepmother and sister were shocked to see her. They had hoped that Baba Yaga would have had Vasilisa for breakfast or lunch and they would be rid of the girl forever. And when Vasilisa didn't appear for a week they were certain that their prayers had been answered.

Poor Vasilisa what a homecoming she had! She was immediately put to the drudgery of work with the three women hurling abuses at her and cursing her for coming back looking lovelier than ever before.

The flaming skull watched the torture of Vasilisa with growing rage.

That night as Vasilisa's step mother and her daughters slept the skull entered their room in the dead of night. It started making ominous sounds which echoed in the still night air. The three women clutched each other unable to even speak. The flaming skull danced around them and as thick long tongues of flame leapt at the three, they died of sheer fright.

Vasilisa and her father lived happily ever after – with Sveta and the flaming skull protecting the two from evil.

# The Legend of Gilgamesh

*(A story from Mesopotamia)*

One of the most fascinating and intriguing mythical heroes of all time is Gilgamesh. According to Mesopotamian mythology Gilgamesh was an early king of Uruk. He was unique because he was two parts god and one part man. The beauty of the Sun God Shamash, shone on his face and the courage of the Storm God, Adad was in his blood.

Though his mother was a woman, he had many divine qualities and supernatural powers. He thus represented a link between Gods and men. In his youth, however, Gilgamesh started misusing his powers. He began acting like a dictator and soon became unpopular with his subjects.

One day the people of Uruk gathered together and prayed to the Gods. "O mighty beings in the heavens above, save us from our ruler. We can no longer bear the torture, the pain and the suffering inflicted upon us by the cruel Gilgamesh!"

The Gods heard the cries for mercy and sat in consultation.

"I feel if Gilgamesh is not controlled he will soon tire of playing around with the lives of the mortals and set his eyes on us Gods," said one God.

"I think the reason why Gilgamesh has become so uncontrollable is because there is absolutely no challenge to him. There is no one who can defy his might."

"Yes, that's right. We should create a rival who is as strong as Gilgamesh. This way his energies would be diverted to his enemy and he would stop torturing his people. And we should also be free from any future threat to us," said Anu, the Sky God.

All the gods agreed and the task of creating a creature equal in might to Gilgamesh was given to Anu and Ninlil, the Mother Goddess.

The two of them created a mirror image of Gilgamesh from clay. They gave the creature life and named it Enkidu. They sent a dream to Gilgamesh announcing the arrival of his rival Enkidu.

Anu and Ninlil dropped Enkidu in the wilderness where he lived and ate like an animal. He became the ruler of the jungle and was soon as powerful and dangerous in the world of nature as Gilgamesh was in the world of men.

Gilgamesh sent a cunning but beautiful woman to tame the wild and unruly Enkidu. She spent a week with him teaching Enkidu how to eat, dress and conduct himself in civilised society. She then took him to Uruk where everyone was amazed at his likeness to the great Gilgamesh.

Enkidu's path crossed with that of the king when Gilgamesh was setting off on one of his missions to loot and plunder. Enkidu challenged Gilgamesh who readily accepted. The fight was glorious – full of awe-inspiring deeds and destruction. The two mighty fighters seemed evenly matched with neither prevailing over the other. Finally Gilgamesh succeeded in tossing his adversary to the ground and overpowering him. At this stage something happened which the gods had not anticipated. They had created Enkidu as the mirror image but had not put in him the divine portion. Due to this the arrogance in Gilgamesh had been replaced by humility in Enkidu. As a result after being vanquished by Gilgamesh, Enkidu accepted defeat with grace and dignity. Gilgamesh welcomed him as his friend and soon Enkidu became the King's most trusted companion.

With Enkidu beside him, Gilgamesh prepared for his greatest adventure yet. He prayed to Shamash, the Sun god, like never before. Pleased, the Sun god gave him the most powerful weapons which man had ever known. Armed with these Gilgamesh and Enkidu set off on their expedition to the divine mountain. This place was covered by magnificent forest of cedar trees and was guarded by a monster called Humbaba, who radiated seven kinds of savage glory.

Shamash sent the Wind god to immobilise Humbaba and Gilgamesh stripped the monster of his magic weapons and beheaded him.

Goddess Ishtar witnessed the bravery of Gilgamesh and fell in love with him. However, Gilgamesh not only spurned but also humiliated her and she was furious. Ishtar went to the gods demanding revenge.

The Gods created the Bull of Heaven and commanded it to kill Gilgamesh and Enkidu. The two heroes destroyed the Bull.

The Gods now were terribly enraged. There was a furious argument as to which of the two was to be punished. Finally it was decided that Enkidu had to die.

Cursed by the Gods, Enkidu died but not as a warrior in the battle field - a death which he would have welcomed. Instead he was struck by a fever and he wasted away. Gilgamesh, the mightiest warrior in the world, who had challenged the heavens and the gods with the might of his arm and the power of his will, could not bear the sorrow of his faithful friend's death.

Gilgamesh gave Enkidu a hero's farewell and took a pledge to bring him back to life. He travelled through the mountain of the rising sun and arrived at the garden of the gods. He learned that only Utnapishtim and his wife, of all humanity, were graced by the gods with eternal life. He persuaded Ursanabi, ferryman of the dead to take him to the under world where Utnapishtim lived.

On meeting Utnapishtim, Gilgamesh said "O revered soul! I am Gilgamesh, the ruler of Uruk. I have come from the extreme end of the Universe to meet you."

"What is it that you want?" the wise man asked.

"I want to know the secret of immortality so that I can revive my friend Enkidu, who has been killed by the Gods." said Gilgamesh

"Gilgamesh, let me first tell you that nothing in the world is permanent. Everything living must die. And moreover, remember, immortality is a life of boredom." Asked Gilgamesh

"I don't understand. How can immortality bring about boredom?"

"To find an answer to this question go now and come back after a week. But during this period make sure that you do not sleep even a wink."

Gilgamesh returned after a week.

"I am sorry master. As much as I tried, I couldn't keep myself from sleeping."

"I knew that, it is not possible for you or any other human being to go without sleep for long. Now just reflect if a few days of staying awake filled you with boredom and exhaustion, how tiresome and boring would be a life that has no end – that would go on and on like an unfinished night," Utnapishtim said.

Gilgamesh stood with his head bowed trying to understand the words of the great master.

Utnapishtim looked at the King and gently said, "Anyway, since you have come all this way, I will not allow you to go back disappointed. I'll give you a plant to revive your friend," with these words Utnapishtim handed over the delicate looking plant to Gilgamesh.

However, on the way back, a serpent stole the plant and Gilgamesh had to return empty-handed.

Thus, the great Gilgamesh spent the rest of his life accepting his mortal state with the memories of his great friend for company.

# The Bridge of Gods

*(A story from North America)*

This is the tale of a time very long ago when all the people were giants. They mixed freely with gods and were brave and powerful. During this unique age lived a giantess called Loowit. She was a priestess friendly with both the good as well as evil spirit. She had invented a fire making device which she kept hidden in the heart of a mountain which is today called Mount Saint Helens. This mountain was like a tipi(tent) to Loowit. The people knew nothing of her secret invention and thought she created fire by supernatural means.

People came to the door of her tipi and requested her for fire. She gave them a single piece of coal kept inside a clamshell. Each visitor would take this piece and light up his or her village.

However if and when the fire went out in a village no one knew how to strike another. When the weather was good they made their journey to Loowit's tipi. But in winters, when it was too cold to travel they simply waited and suffered in miserable cold.

Sometimes it so happened when the people managed to reach the tipi they went back empty handed. This occurred when Loowit was deep in meditation in some corner in the depth of the huge mountain. The visitors not able to locate her waited and waited and then left without the fire.

Loowit sometimes went around in the guise of an elderly beggar. She saw people suffering without fire. Often fire got extinguished due to rain, wind, flood or some human error. Without fire the humans faced terrible agony- especially in winters.

When Loowit saw all this, she felt really sorry for the people. She thought to herself, "If I show them my magic device each one will be able to make fire. They will not be afraid of cold winters and dark nights and live happily ever after. But once I reveal my secret, will anyone respect me anymore?"

She thought a lot about the pros and cons of teaching people the art of making fire and came to a decision, "Even if they don't care for me it doesn't matter. I have to save my people from this unending misery."

From the invention of fire to her dilemma, many years had passed and Loowit had grown very old. Her cheeks were wrinkled, her eyes tired, her hair was white and her hands withered. In her heart however Loowit had remained young. Caged inside the body of an old and withered woman was a youthful and vibrant girl.

After she had decided to share the secrets of her fire with the people at large, she prayed to Tyhee Saghalie, the Chief of the Gods.

He heard her in his heavenly abode and came striding down the milky way. He was accompanied by his two sons Pahtoe and Wyeast, who lived in the mountains, which later came to be known as Adams and Hood.

Loowit showed Tyhee her invention which was basically a drill that made fire when it was whirled at the right speed. Tyhee, who made fire by hurling thunderbolts, was impressed by Loowit's invention.

"Tyhee, I don't want the people of the world to be dependent on me for fire. This dependence is causing a lot of suffering. I cannot go around distributing my invention to the people. I request you to take my drill, make as many duplicates as are required and give them to the needy" said Loowit.

Tyhee agreed and took the drill. In a moment he had made a duplicate drill. He gave each of his sons one drill, "Take this, make many more and give them to the people telling that this is a gift from the great mountain priestess – Loowit."

He turned towards Loowit and then asked, "Loowit, your concern for others and your selflessness is truly unmatched. Tell me what is it that you want most?"

"I have lost my youth, I want it back," Loowit said.

Tyhee gave Loowit back her youth and beauty. He made her the guardian of the Bridge of the Gods. This magical bridge, it was believed, led directly to the milky way and from there to the country of the Chief of Gods.

"Loowit, there exists two bridges here. One is the physical bridge and the other the spiritual bridge. Those who are giants only in body but have narrow, mean spirits should not be allowed to cross over. Only those who are giants in spirit as well as in body can be allowed to pass through."

Loowit left her abode in the mountain and started living in a small stone house in the middle of the Bride of the Gods. Now Loowit had become so beautiful that many men wanted to marry her. She however refused all of them. The two Princes Pahitoe and Wyeast who had been impressed with her largeness of heart were now struck by her comeliness. Each decide to make her his wife.

She told them with great politeness, "I am honoured by your offer of marriage. However, I cannot accept. I have decided to lead the life of an ascetic and no one can change my mind."

The Princes spoke among themselves. "If she will not decide between us, we will fight each other. Whoever wins will marry her by force."

Having decided this the Princes took on each other. They were powerful Princes and their battle created an upheaval which had never earlier been seen. They used hurricanes and bolts of lightening against one another and the battled raged on.

Finally on the Bridge of the Gods as the Princes grappled with each other using their fearsome strength to the full, the unthinkable happened.

'The Bridge of the Gods' collapsed into the Wauna river.

Hearing the sound of the crash Tyhee came striding down his eyes blazing.

He picked up Wyest and Pahtoe and fixed them in the heart of Mount Hood and Mount Adams.

Loowit sat on the edge of Wauna river looking at the ruins of the bridge.

"Now I am the guardian neither of the fire nor of the Bridge. O Tyhee! I will go back to the dark regions of the mountain and hide in the black depths. I will never go out and mix with people so that my beauty will never again cause any destruction," she lamented, tears flowing from her beautiful eyes.

"Loowit, the spirit of The Bridge of Gods exists within you. Only the physical bridge is ruined. I have reduced the size of humanity so that no one may cause the kind of destruction my sons have. However, the hearts of people I have not changed. Some will have great hearts, some will have small ones."

Tyhee looked at Loowit and with a gentle smile continued, "When I direct you Loowit, you will unfold the Spirit Bridge for those of the earth who are large of heart. But for those who are mean minded with little hearts this great bridge will remain closed. And if future generations break my laws and create havoc you will have the power to break even this Spirit Bridge and thereby prevent anyone from reaching my abode – the Country of the Gods."

# How Music Came to Earth

*(A story from Mexico)*

Tezcatlipoca (we'll call him Tez to give our tongues some relief) was the 'God of heaven and of the four quarters of the heavens'. He came to earth and was very sad at the state of affairs. One day he sent word for Quetzalcoatl, the Wind God. The Wind, which was scattered all over the earth, rose high in the air. Whipping the waters of the oceans and the manes of the trees he arrived at the feet of Tez.

"Wind, the earth is sick from silence. We possess light, colour, flowers, fruits and other bounties of nature but alas we have no music." said Tez

The Wind bowed his head sharing the sadness of heaven.

"We must bestow music on all creation," Tez declared slipping into verse,

*"To the awakening dawn,*
*to the dreaming man*
*to the waiting mother*
*to the passing water and*
*to the flying bird*
*Life should be all music."*

*The Wind swayed in agreement.*

"Go then through the boundless sadness to the high house of the Sun. Father Sun is surrounded by makers of music who play their flutes sweetly and scatter light. Bring back to the earth some of these musicians," Tez ordered.

The Wind, using all his considerable speed and strength, went up, leaving the earth in silence. He continued travelling till he reached the heavenly roof of the world where all melodies lived in a nest of light. On reaching his destination, wind found that the Sun's musicians were clad in four colours. Each colour represented a different theme. *White* was for *lullabies*, *red* for *epic poems*, *yellow* for *golden melodies* and *blue* for the *tales of the wandering poets*. All the musicians were guided by the Sun from the peaks of the world.

The musicians were bright and cheerful and there was no place for the colours of darkness and gloom.

When the Sun saw the Wind approaching he told his musicians, "Here comes the bothersome Wind from the earth. Stop your music and your songs. Don't pay any heed to him. Whoever responds to the wind will have to go back with him to the silence of the earth."

The Wind addressed the musicians, "Come on O' melody makers." There was complete silence. The wind raised his voice, "Musicians, singers, the supreme lord of the world is calling you."

There was still no response. Tez, the God of heaven, who was watching this drama swung into action. Dark, wicked clouds, spurred on by streaks of lightening besieged the house of the Sun. The fury unleashed by Tez, overpowered the Sun completely. Terrified the musicians and singers ran for shelter and landed straight in the lap of the Wind. The Wind held them gently, making sure he didn't harm their tender melodies. He set off with them on his downward journey to the earth, happy at the success of his mission.

Below, the earth raised its wide dark eyes to heaven and its great face shone with happiness. The branches of the trees, the wings of the birds, the face of the flowers and the cheeks of the fruits welcomed the musicians.

The melody makers spread to the four quarters, caressing the valleys, the forests and the seas. Music was born in the bosom of the earth. Thus all things learn to sing:

*The awakening dawn,*
*the dreaming man*
*the waiting mother*
*the passing water and*
*the flying bird.*

And life was music from that time on.

# The Adventures of Theseus

*(A story from Greece)*

Aegeus the great king of Athens once visited a city in Southern Greece. There he met a beautiful woman, whose name was Aethra, and married her. After some time he decided to come back to Athens leaving his wife behind. Before he left he placed a sword in a hollow and covered it with a huge stone.

"You are going to be blessed with a child. If the child is a boy, then when he grows ask him to shift this stone. If he is strong enough to do it let him pick up this sword and come to Athens and meet me. I shall be waiting for him.

In due course a male child was born to the woman whom Aegeus had abandoned. He was named Theseus. He grew up big and strong and brave. One day his mother took him to the stone and he shifted it quite easily.

"Pick up the sword and go to your father in Athens," she told him.

Theseus had the choice of going by ship or road. The voyage by sea was an easier option free from dangers, while the one by road was full of challenges. Theseus being brave and adventurous, took off by road, not heeding the advice of elders.

On the way he encountered robbers and monsters who plagued the roads. One of them called Periphetes had an iron club which Theseus seized and bludgeoned the giant to death. Another monster

called Sinis was famous for killing his victims by tying them between two pine trees. He would then bend the pine trees backwards to the ground and release them. The pine trees would spring up tearing the victims apart. Theseus did exactly the same with Sinis and the monster was killed.

Polypemon Procrustes was a giant who placed his victims on an iron bed. He would then chop them if their bodies were longer than the bed or stretch them if their bodies were shorter. In either case the victims died a gruesome death. Theseus, using his immense strength and cunning turned the table on Procrustes and killed him in exactly the same manner.

Cercyon was a wrestler who gained strength from the earth. Theseus lifted him in the air thereby sapping the monster's energy. He then easily killed him.

By the time Theseus reached Athens his fame had spread. Aegeus invited the brave young man to a banquet without knowing that Theseus was his son. The King fearing competition from Theseus decided to kill him. As the cup of poison was handed over to him Theseus drew his sword. Aegeus immediately recognised his sword and seizing the cup from his son's hand threw it away.

Aegeus then embraced his son and declared to the people of Athens that Theseus was his son and heir.

It was not long before Theseus got an opportunity to display his valour to the people of Athens. Crete was a kingdom ruled by Minos a powerful and autocratic king. His only son Androgeus came on a visit to Athens. Aegeus sent him on a dangerous expedition to kill a fierce bull. Unfortunately Androgeus was killed in the fight. When Minos came to know he was mad with rage and attacking Athens, captured it. He then threatened to destroy the city completely. Aegeus, who was now repenting for inviting this disaster on Athens, begged Minos to spare the city.

"I shall spare you and your kingdom only on one condition. Every year you have to send seven young men and women to me."

Aegeus had no choice but to agree.

The men and women who went to Crete all met with the same fate. They were given to Minotaur, the son of Minos. Minotaur, a monster who was half man, half bull was kept in a labyrinth from which it was impossible to escape.

When Theseus came to know of this practice he told his father, "I shall go in place of one of the victims."

Aegeus tried to reason with him but Theseus was adamant. "Don't worry father, have confidence in me. I'll kill that monster and release Athens from his curse forever."

As he was getting into the ship, Theseus reassured his father, "This ship carries a black sail. When I come back after killing the Minotaur, I'll change the sail to white so you'll get the good news much before I have landed."

When the victims arrived the people of Crete lined up to have a look. Among them was Adriane, the daughter of Minos. She looked at Theseus and fell in love with the handsome young man. Adriane sent a message to Theseus, "I will help you get out of the labyrinth if you promise to take me with you to Athens and marry me."

Theseus agreed and Adriane secretly gave him a ball of thread. "You tie one end to the door of the labyrinth and unwind the ball as you proceed. On your way back, all you have to do is to follow the thread and you'll be back at the entrance."

Theseus walked in to the labyrinth following Adriane's instructions. At the end of the maze was the terrible Minotaur. The huge and fearsome monster attacked Theseus with a fury he had never faced. The brave, young man fought back with equal strength and greater agility. The battle raged on and on with neither fighter willing to give up easily. Finally Theseus managed to push the Minotaur on the ground and killed him.

Theseus followed the thread and was soon out of the labyrinth.

While his companions greeted him with joy Adriane's warned him. "You were to only escape from Minotaur's clutches not kill him. That monster is the son of Minos and the king will not spare you. If we do not flee Crete immediately we shall all be killed."

The young men and women accompanied by Theseus and Adriane sailed back before Minos realised what had happened.

On the way back, Theseus and his companions stopped to take rest on an island named Naxos. There while Adriane was asleep, Theseus left for Athens. At that point of time Theseus committed a major blunder. He forgot to replace the black sail with a white one. Aegeus, who had been watching the sea every day, saw the black sail and assumed the worst.

"Alas! My son has been killed. What is the point now in my living," with these words of lament he flung himself from a precipice into the sea and died.

Whether Aegeus had to pay for abandoning his wife and unborn son is a question worth thinking over.

After his father's tragic death Theseus was crowned the king of Athens. He ruled his kingdom wisely and well and Athens became a rich and prosperous kingdom.

# Urvashi

*(A story from India)*

A long time ago lived two princesses - Urvashi and Deepa. They were the daughters of Prashant Dev, the King of Devnagar. Urvashi, the elder one was very beautiful, intelligent and talented. Trained in classical music, she was easily the most gifted singer in the land. In the game of chess there was no one who could beat her; not even the King who was himself an accomplished player. In sword fighting too, her skill, agility and nimbleness made her the best.

However, there was one bad quality that overshadowed her talent, brilliance and beauty. This quality was her pride and it had made Urvashi arrogant, selfish and cruel.

Deepa on the other hand was quite the opposite of Urvashi. She was neither as beautiful nor as talented as Urvashi. But she was modest, kind and loving. The King was very fond of Urvashi but the people adored only Deepa.

One day the King called Urvashi to his chamber and told her, "Urvashi dear, you are now 19. You should think about getting married.

"Father I have made up my mind how I am going to go about it. You will have to organise a swayamvar and send invitations all over the country to various kings and princes. There will be a competition and the winner will win my hand in marriage."

"That's a wonderful idea. Let them compete with each other to decide the most eligible man." Agreed the king.

"Not with each other, they will have to compete with me."

"But why?" Asked the king.

"If they compete with each other how will I know if the winner is suitable for me." Replied Urvashi.

"What a brilliant idea! But if you have to compete with every suitor will it not be very boring and tiring for you?" The king asked.

"I have thought of that too. Before the competition father, you will have to make an announcement that the loser will have to become my slave for a year and spend this period in the royal prison. This will dissuade most and only the men who have confidence in themselves will remain."

The preparations began in real earnest immediately. Messengers were rushed to all corners of the country with the invitation. Urvashi had chosen three events. The suitors had to compete with her in sword fighting, chess and music and beat her in all the events. The competitors were given six months to prepare themselves.

The competition was conducted in the royal stadium with more than half the kingdom turning out to watch the contest.

Some of the suitors managed to beat her in the game of chess while others in sword fighting. A few were better than her in singing. But there was not a single king or prince who could outshine her in all the three events. As a result within two weeks 44 kings and princes became Urvashi's slaves. Their duty was to work in the fields like common labourers during the day and spend their nights in the dungeons.

Six months went by. The number of suitors reduced to a trickle and then completely stopped.

A few days later a young man presented himself before the King. He was tall and well built. There was a kind of glow on his face and he appeared extremely confident of himself.

"Who are you and what do you want?" Asked the king.

"I am Karan. I come from Krantipur. I want to compete with the princess." Replied the man.

"Are you the king of Krantipur or his son?" Urvashi asked. She had the feeling that here at last was a man who could compete with her on equal terms and possibly even defeat her.

"Neither. I am the son of a cobbler."

"How dare you come here, you mochi? How can you even imagine competing with me when even kings and princes of royal blood have tasted nothing but defeat."

"Princess, I thought the contest was about talent, skill and intelligence - not about caste and lineage. Are you scared of losing out to the son of a mochi?"

"No, of course not!" Urvashi shouted, her eyes blazing. I'll allow you to compete with me. And when you lose I'll get you thrown in a pit full of crocodiles. Do you agree or you want to chicken out?"

"Princess, please rephrase your words; it is not when I lose, but if I lose," Karan replied.

Soon the news of the contest spread far and wide. People came from different parts of the kingdom as well as the neighbouring kingdoms to watch the contest between the beautiful princess and the handsome commoner in the royal stadium.

The first event was the sword fight. If Urvashi was good, Karan was brilliant. Within seconds he unarmed Urvashi and the entire stadium burst into thunderous applause.

The second event was the game of chess. In 21 moves Karan checkmated Urvashi to the delight of the huge crowd.

The third and final competition was the next evening, in the royal gardens. The music contest began with Urvashi singing the Deepak raga. Such was the power of her music that one by one all the lamps lit up on their own.

Karan responded by singing the Megh Malhar. All of a sudden clouds appeared in the clear blue evening sky and it started raining.

Urvashi sang a lilting melody and beautiful peacocks came gambolling from the nearby forests. Karan sang an equally melodious raga and the peacocks started dancing. It was a beautiful sight - a dozen or more peacocks dancing in perfect rhythm to Karan's song.

The contest went on and on. Finally Karan declared, "Princess, I think we have had enough fun. Now I would like to settle the issue. Please arrange for an animal that has died in the last twenty four hours.

A dead deer was brought to him. He placed the deer's head in his lap and started singing. He went on and on for almost an hour. Slowly the deer opened its eyes, stirred and raised its head. Karan who was by now sweating profusely raised the pitch of his song. His eyes were closed and his face a picture of concentration. The deer licked his face and getting up hobbled off into the jungle. The onlookers went crazy. They had never seen this kind of a miracle. They got up and began applauding.

Karan took a bow and then looking at the princess said "Now princess, can you do this?"

Urvashi just watched mesmerised. She couldn't believe her eyes. Karan wasn't merely a singer he was a magician. Urvashi knew she was a great singer but she couldn't work miracles. She got up and declared, "My dear citizens of Devnagar. For the first time in my life I have to admit that there is someone who is better than me. I have no hesitation in acknowledging defeat. I am ready and willing to marry this handsome, intelligent and talented young man."

The applause was deafening.

"But I am not," Karan's voice rang out loud and clear.

"What?" Urvashi asked quite sure she hadn't heard right.

"Princess, I am not interested in marrying you." There was a stunned silence.

"Then why in heaven's name did you come to Devnagar and participate in the contest?"

"To teach you a lesson, to break your pride and to prove to you that you are not the greatest. I think Princess I owe it to you and Maharaj to tell you the full story behind my coming here. Arjun Singh, the Prince of Krantipur is my best friend. Even though he is a prince and I am a commoner he has always treated me like his own brother. Arjun set his eyes on the Princess at a fair, a couple of years ago and fell in love with her. When he came to know of the swayamvar he began practising hard. When he competed with the Princess he beat her in chess and was her equal in classical music. When it came to sword fighting he was having the upper hand till the last round. As the fight reached its climax he held back a little because he was scared of hurting her. His love for Urvashi was so great that he felt it was better he admit defeat rather than cause her even the slightest injury. As a result he lost the contest and was thrown in the dungeons. He couldn't bear the humiliation and the torture and was driven almost insane. An angel of mercy saw him in this state and took him under her care. She nursed him back to health and quietly sent him back to the dungeons because she didn't want to interfere with your judgment or the King's decision.

When I came to know of my friend's predicament I came here to see him. I met the angel of mercy and fell in love with her. I proposed to her and she accepted even though she is of royal lineage and I am a cobbler's son. I told her she would have to leave her palatial house and live with me in my humble abode. I teach sword fighting and music and earn a decent living but I would never be able to offer her the luxury she has been used to. She heard me patiently and then replied, "Your love is more important to me than all the comforts and riches of the world."

"Who are you talking about?" Urvashi said her voice barely a whisper.

" It's Deepa your younger sister. I love her and want to marry her."

"I don't believe it. She is no match for me. No sane man can prefer her over me. You are doing it only to take spite on me."

"Princess Urvashi, it is this arrogance which is your greatest shortcoming. You are beautiful, talented, intelligent but you lack qualities which endear one human being to the other."

"What qualities?" Asked Urvashi

"A kind, loving and merciful heart. A soul which cares for the feelings of others and a mind that is not absorbed completely in itself." Replied Karan.

Urvashi did not utter a word; she simply got up and walked out of the royal garden.

Karan looked at the King. "Maharaj, will you give me your daughter Princess Deepa's hand in marriage."

"I have no objection if Deepa is willing." Replied the king.

Deepa had just entered the royal garden. The King asked her and bowing her head she nodded shyly.

Later Karan told the King. "Maharaj, I want to take my friend Arjun with me."

"Son, I talked to the panditjee he has fixed next Friday as the day of the wedding. I will release Arjun and all the other prisoners well in time so that they attend the wedding.

Two nights later Arjun was sleeping in one of the dungeons when he heard someone whispering. He opened his eyes and looked around. Huddled in one corner, a few of the slaves were discussing.

"Everything is ready. I have bribed one of the guards. Exactly at the stroke of midnight he will open the gate of the dungeon and show us the passage that will directly lead to Princess Urvashi's chamber. It is guarded by six armed guards."

"But we are unarmed," said one of the prisoner.

"You don't have to worry about that. On the walls lining the staircase ornamental swords are hanging. We have to just pick them up and charge. Don't forget we are twenty in number."

"Good. For six months I have been waiting for this day. I want to chop the beautiful Princess, pretty head off," snarled one of the 'slaves'. Arjun recognised him. He was Gajendra, the Prince of Gajrajnagar, who had lost to the Princess in all the three rounds.

"We all want to extract our revenge Gajendra," chorused the others.

As he heard their plan, Arjun's heart turned icy cold. Even though, Urvashi had caused him so much misery and torture he still loved her with all his heart.

Arjun slipped out along with the others at twelve. He knew the way to Urvashi's palace. He raced ahead and entered Urvashi's chamber.

"Quick, the slaves have escaped. They are coming here to slaughter the Princess," he whispered to the guards. He grabbed the sword hanging on the wall and turned around to face the attackers. A few seconds later the prisoners pounced on Arjun and the guards, like enraged beasts. Within a few minutes, all the guards were killed and it was left to Arjun, to face fourteen armed prisoners. He was an expert in sword fighting and kept the marauders at bay. In the meantime, Urvashi was woken up. She came out, sword in hand and the two of them beat back the attackers. Soon, the King's guards arrived and the prisoners were taken into custody. Urvashi turned around to thank Arjun and found him lying in a heap, bleeding profusely. Arjun was taken to the Princess' chamber.

"The Prince has been very seriously injured and has suffered severe blood loss. He needs complete rest and care," the doctor said.

Urvashi looked at the handsome Prince lying with his eyes closed and his body swathed completely in bandages. The person she had publicly humiliated, and thrown into the dungeons, had ultimately risked his life to save hers.

For the next three days and three nights, Urvashi spent every moment taking care of the Prince.

Two days before the royal wedding, Arjun and Urvashi were sitting in the royal garden.

"Princess I don't know how to thank you for your care and concern," Arjun said.

"Please Arjun, don't embarrass me further. What I did was my duty. But what you did was your greatness. You risked your life to save mine. I don't know how I'll ever be able to repay you."

"I wouldn't use the word repayment Urvashi, but there is one way you can make me the happiest man in the whole wide world."

"How?"

"By consenting to marry me," Arjun said, taking Urvashi's hand in his.

"I will marry you," she replied.

Tales, Folk Tales & Legends
GOOD BOOKS
SATISFACTION GUARANTEED
Affordable Prices
Tales of Gopal the jester
Full of Wit, Wisdom & Humour
60/- each
60/- each
Folk Tales
50/- each
Enchanting Fairy Tales
50/- each
Tenali Rama
60/- each
Tales of Tenali Rama
60/- each
71 Golden Tales of Panchatantra
60/- each
5 Volumes + Combined Edition Also available in Hindi
350/- H.B.
The Great Adventure of Lav Kush
36/- each
PANDA
An imprint of Unicorn Books, Delhi
Quality reading for children...
Indian Tales & Global Tales, New Tales & Folk Tales, Fables, Legends & Mythology and books on growing up well, first told or retold by children's authors.
All Books in Full Colour
Animal Folk Tales from Around the World
36/- each
3 Volumes. Also available in Hindi
Other Story Books
50 Wittiest Tales of BIRBAL
48/-
30/-
Interesting Stories to Learn PROVERBS
72/-
In Colour
80/-
50 Moral Tales ...from The Gurukul
68/-
In Colour
68/-
In Colour
Ancient Tales of Wit, Wisdom & Humour
48/-
The Funniest Tales of Mullah Nasruddin
48/- each
JATAKA TALES
48/-
30/-
Great News Guys!
You now have your very own corner in cyberspace:
www.kidscorner.com
UNICORN BOOKS
J-3/16, Daryaganj, New Delhi-110002.
Tel: 23276539, 23272783-84
E-mail: unicornbooks@vsnl.com